The Book of Rodney

Satan Sometimes

Brings Cupcakes

Angelica Asher

Edition: November 2020

ISBN 978-0-9629-5559-4

The Book of Rodney is a work of fiction. Names, characters, places, and incidents are a product of the author's imagination. Any resemblance to actual people, living or dead, or places, is completely coincidental.

Cover photo by Matthew Fried.

Published by Benjamin, Ross and Lane
www.BenjaminRossLane.com

Please visit the author's official website at www.AngelicaAsher.com.

Chapter 1

*Then he dreamed, and behold, a ladder was set up on the
earth, and its top reached to heaven;
and there the angels of God were ascending
and descending on it.*

~ Genesis 28:12

He didn't know this, of course, because angels can't see into
the future or read men's minds, but Adoram was about to
have his even-keeled existence upended by a clumsy red-headed
teenager. Adoram headed to earth regularly to check up on the
guardian angels he oversaw, going by way of many of the same
portals that he had been using for hundreds of years. True, some
new ones had been created since Adoram first started his job as a
supervising angel a millennium ago—mostly in Africa, China and
north America.

Today, Adoram fluttered his six wings and they gently
propelled him through the heavenly streets of gold, down an alley,
over to a field where ten or so other angels were lined up waiting
to access a newer portal to the physical dimension. Some of the

angels were four-winged, some had six wings, and some had two. All of them were dressed in pure white linen robes. Along some of the robes, from the shoulder to the waist, ran golden sashes. If one didn't know better, this scene might have been mistaken for an odd beauty contest.

Adoram joined the back of the line and watched the other angels climb onto the glowing ladder which resembled a twisting DNA helix. As the angels descended a few rungs, they disappeared from their spiritual dimension and appeared on earth at a corresponding spot in Los Angeles. When it was his turn to descend, Adoram fluttered his wings slightly and grabbed the ladder. His seraph angel feet felt the change first as they moved down the rungs. It was a bit like being shocked by a low voltage wire, stimulating but not too painful. Adoram knew from experience that this particular transition zone was only about 15 rungs deep, making one full twist of the ladder. This portal, or HeavenLink as the angels called it, was located closest to his appointment on earth. He used it every April to give dominion angel Barook his annual review.

As he materialized on earth that beautiful, warm, spring day, Adoram fluttered his wings again and flew quickly off the ladder onto the ground. Sulphur dioxide and diesel fumes from the L.A. traffic registered in the angel's nose. The Los Angeles HeavenLink was obscured behind some bushes at the back of Angelus Temple in Echo Park, a downtown neighborhood. Not that it needed to be hidden. Most people couldn't detect a

HeavenLink with their physical senses. Adoram cleared the ladder and took a minute to watch the angels behind him fly toward their duties in the city. They flew in all directions: some went north toward Glendale. Others went south toward Compton. And still others flew off west toward the sea. Adoram headed northwest into the San Fernando Valley where he knew guardian angel Barook was looking after his oh-so-clumsy personal assignment.

Once Adoram reached the city of Van Nuys, he flew along Sherman Way and whooshed past latecomers straggling in through the doors of The Church on the Way like cows coming home to the barn after a full day of grazing. The Church's pastor, Jack Temple, was animatedly reading from the book of Ephesians while traversing the stage that served as a pulpit. He was like Steve Harvey delivering a monologue. Adoram stopped for a moment near the ceiling so he could watch the passionate preacher deliver his message.

"Finally, my brethren, be strong in the Lord and in the power of His might. Put on the whole armor of God that you may be able to stand against the wiles of the devil."

Hovering over a row of churchgoers, Adoram looked down at the men and women dressed in their Sunday-go-to-meetin' clothes. He nodded at dominion angel Clovis who was sitting next to an elderly woman whose stomach kept growling. Adoram saw a demon in the form of a capuchin monkey clinging to the old woman's shoulder. The monkey whispered into her ear, "You're so hungry. What should you have for lunch when this is over? How about fried chicken? You love fried chicken." The woman licked her lips dreamily as Clovis leaned over and whispered in her other ear, "Listen, this is the good part of the sermon."

"For we do not wrestle against flesh and blood but against principalities, against powers, against the rulers of the darkness of this age, against spiritual hosts of wickedness."

Adoram winked at Clovis and passed on over the heads of the congregation. He could see winged dominion angels sitting next to their charges or hovering just above them. He also clocked the number of demonic creatures everywhere, attempting to distract and annoy the people there—too many of them for Adoram's liking.

Pastor Temple raised his arms above his head and continued, "Therefore take up the whole armor of God" as the seraph angel glided elegantly out the doors and across the courtyard where the classrooms were located. Through the windows of one of the classrooms, he noted Rodney Simplessohn arranging used furniture into rows and aisles. On the wall outside the room, a sign hung:

Church Bazaar Today!

Come Explore the Treasures of the Kingdom!

And Other Used Stuff.

Proceeds Benefit our Outreach Ministries.

Rodney could hear Pastor Temple delivering his sermon through the sound system. "Are you a spiritual warrior," he asked his church congregants, "or a spiritual wimp?"

"I'm probably a spiritual wimp," Rodney replied to the crackling speaker mounted on the wall as his skinny arms strained to pick up a shabby side table that reeked of paint stripper.

"Let me now share a truth with you that I learned from my friend Pastor Joseph Prince from Singapore," Pastor Temple continued. "God has an armor. It is what Jesus wore when He walked on earth. He left the armor behind for us when He returned to heaven. That armor is recognizable to Satan. Remember the medieval knights you learned about in school? They wore armor that identified them, too. Their shields and helmets bore their family crests. Each knight's armor was made a certain way, customized for them. It was recognizable to the crowds who were cheering them on. Well, Satan knows God's armor well. And when you put on God's armor, all the devil sees is God—not you. Isn't that amazing? Satan sees the armor that defeated him 2,000 years ago at the cross."

Shadowing Rodney like a loyal guard dog was dominion angel Barook, dressed in the uniform of all the angels: a white linen robe. His two feathery white wings splayed out from his shoulders and hung down to his thighs. Barook was seriously concentrating with all his might on the lanky, freckle-faced young man in front of him.

"Greetings, Barook," whispered Adoram.

Barook looked up and smiled at his old friend. "Huzzah! Tis thee! Has the time come again so soon, for my angelic review? Why, it seems as though the golden wheat has felt the sickle but once since last we met."

Adoram enjoyed the antiquated way that Barook spoke. Barook was one of the oldest angels and he took his time adjusting his language over the centuries. It was endearing.

"That's probably because you're so focused on your charge there." Adoram nodded toward Rodney who was at that moment stumbling around while attempting to carry a very old, very huge television set. Barook spread his hands out like a basketball player guarding an opponent and followed behind the swaying, weaving, red-haired eighteen-year-old in an attempt to protect him.

"I can see the challenges you face with your current assignment haven't eased up in the past year. And yet, he bears no fresh scars. Well done."

"I givest thou my humblest thanks," responded Barook while barely removing his eyes from Rodney who was now pulling a giant exercise ball out of a pile of sports equipment. A fishing rod and a skateboard went in two different directions as Rodney yanked the ball loose, falling backwards. Barook was there, instantly, underneath Rodney to absorb the blow when the boy hit the floor. "Ooomph," they uttered in unison.

"I hate to pull you away from your duties, even for a second, but I need your seal on this angelic review," said Adoram. "I'm giving you five halos."

Before Adoram had finished speaking, Rodney was on the move again, bouncing his way down each aisle on the exercise ball instead of walking.

"Thank you, sir, but canst thou know the depth and breadth of energy flow from that boy so seeming slow?" asked Barook in his old-fashioned vernacular. "He is not allowed to go near that paper you hold just so—that slice of spirit, piece of heaven, home of God. This thou knowest well, I'm sure, but please move farther from that boy."

"Ah, I see. Is this far enough away?" asked Adoram from the corner of the room.

"Perhaps this ritual we should conduct up near the ceiling, sir."

"Really? Well that would be fine," answered Adoram as he floated up and unrolled the angelic scroll.

Below them, Rodney accidentally rode his bouncing FitBall onto the errant skateboard.

Not noticing the antics of the teenager below, Barook pressed his thumb onto the document as his signature in unison with Adoram. The document glowed under the power of the angels' touch. At that same moment, the ball-topped skateboard propelled Rodney onto a mini trampoline below the winged creatures. Rodney bounced up off the trampoline and shot skyward at an alarming rate. He took on the supernatural white glow of the document as he passed through it and hit the ceiling with a thud. "Ohhhhhh!" he cried.

Horrified, Barook instantly flew to the floor to absorb Rodney's inevitable crash. As Rodney neared the concrete floor, Barook's wings guided the boy onto a pile of soft, worn-out clothes. Rodney had the wind knocked out of him, but nothing worse.

"Oh dear!" exclaimed Adoram, afraid of the glow that Rodney had taken on when he sailed through the powered angelic contract. "I wonder what that means."

∬∬

Rodney very slowly unwound himself from the crumpled heap his arms and legs had become. He watched the FitBall bounce away in one direction and the skateboard roll away in another. Behind him he did a double-take at the trampoline. "Wow! That was fire!" Whipping his head around he shouted, "Hey Kirby, did you see that?"

Kirby, another teenager volunteering in the church's rummage sale for the day, stood up from where he had been stooping behind the cashier's desk. "See what?"

"Oh, man," said Rodney. "It was an epic wipeout. You didn't get that on camera?"

"No, dude. I missed the whole thing. I'm going for some coffee. I'll be right back. Hold down the fort."

Barook was just picking himself up off the floor when Rodney noticed him.

"Oh no! Did I plow into you?" Rodney asked with concern.

Barook continued examining Rodney for any visible signs of injury without acknowledging the boy's question.

Just then, Adoram descended from the ceiling to assess the situation.

"Howdy, ma'am," said Rodney. "I'm really shook right now. I had a pretty wicked fall. You're a little blurry, as a matter of fact. Did I hurt you? Or this nice woman over here? She was on the ground a minute ago."

"No, no, we're fine. Thank you, young man," answered Adoram while Barook's face took on an expression of understanding and terror.

"Oh, good," said Rodney. He wondered why the lady in front of him, wearing a long white dress, had such a deep voice. Then he wondered why the other lady was dressed the same way. He tried to focus on the fluttering things attached to their backs, but the eye can't always see what the brain can't comprehend.

"Didst thou hearest?" gasped Barook, backing away from Rodney, his wings quivering.

"I did. This is not good," Adoram replied.

"It's not that bad," chirped Rodney, answering the angel he shouldn't have been able to hear. "I'll be fine. I just need to sit down for a minute."

Adoram joined Barook in backing out of the room while Barook whispered, "He can seest our faces. He can hearest our voices. Woe unto us! Woe unto him!"

"Perhaps it's not that bad. This must have happened before in the history of humanity," responded Adoram. "Surely this can't be the first time such an accident has occurred. I'll go back to heaven right now and find out. Stay with him, but not as close as usual. Try to blend in with the people until I get back with some news." Adoram bolted out the door and immediately took flight on his route back through the valley and towards the HeavenLink downtown.

Barook, left standing in the doorway wondering what to do, stared at Rodney as the lad made his way to an old pink velvet couch lightly perfumed with a mélange of dog pee and mothballs. "You must be really anxious to buy something," Rodney offered in the way of conversation. "Kirby will be right back. He's just getting some coffee."

Barook stared at Rodney without saying a word. The angel wasn't a big talker. He liked to play a more physical role with his charges. He preferred protecting clumsy folks who didn't need a lot of verbal advice. "Ahem, yes, sir. I am anxious to purchase baskets fine for a tiny donkey of mine."

"You have a donkey? How cool is that?" Rodney beamed.

"Tis the height and breadth of cool, the complete sum and pinnacle," Barook stammered.

♫♫♫♫

Adoram climbed up the glowing ladder and—poof! He was home. The seraph angel unfurled his six wings and used them to navigate toward archangel Gabriel's office. He flew down golden streets, past gates made of gemstones, and past the crystal temple of God in which God was seated on His holy throne amid flashings of lightning and fire, encircled by a glorious rainbow. Adoram flew down a small cobblestoned street that resembled a quaint English town in the countryside. He landed just before a tiny white gate. Walking through it, a gardenia bush with an abundance of small white blooms caught his eye. He took a moment to inhale deeply. Adoram approached the door of what appeared to be a tiny cottage.

A knock on the door with a brass knocker in the shape of a cow's head summoned a wingless dominion angel. Adoram explained that he didn't have an appointment, but urgently needed to speak with Gabriel. The dominion angel opened the door wide to admit Adoram. A huge entryway became apparent behind him. He was now standing in the foyer of a huge English manor house, complete with crystal chandeliers and a double marble staircase winding toward a massive landing on the second floor. Gabriel had built the best of both worlds: it had the charm of a country cottage on the outside and the space and grandeur of a palace on the inside.

Eventually Adoram was shown into Gabriel's office. An enormous, intricately carved mahogany desk sat in front of very tall windows. Gabriel stood up to greet his old friend, towering almost 18 feet high as he did so. His wingless body glimmered like a gemstone as he walked around from behind his desk to greet his unexpected visitor.

"Adoram. It's been too long. I've missed you." He bent down and grasped his friend's hands warmly. "But I doubt you are here for a social call."

"No, I'm not," said Adoram bending backward in order to look up at his superior. "One of the people on earth—a believer— has suddenly developed the ability to see spiritual beings. I thought you should know right away. And I'm hoping you can give me some advice on how to help him deal with this, this—," he searched for the right word, "situation."

"Oh my. *Geisterseherkraft* has returned," said Gabriel, crossing his arms in front of his chest. Have a seat." He pointed to a large couch behind a coffee table set up with tea service. "Tea?"

"No, thank you. What is that you said?" asked Adoram, fluttering his wings a bit in order to reach the high couch, and settling down on it.

"That's what Martin Luther called it. '*Geisterseherkraft'* means the ability to see spirits. How did it occur?" Gabriel sat next to him.

"Well, it involved a skateboard and a huge bouncy ball and a mini trampoline, I think. His guardian angel Barook and I were—on the ceiling mind you—almost finished sealing Barook's performance review when suddenly his teenage charge, Rodney Simplessohn, came flying toward us and right through the angelic contract while it was still glowing."

"Oh my," said Gabriel. "The ceiling you say? That's a new one. Well, this type of vision has happened in people before, but it doesn't usually go well for the person. Since he's a Christian, he has a firmer foundation than most humans. But *geisterseherkraft* can really unhinge people. Break the news to him gently. Explain it as well as you can. And try to keep Satan from finding out. He'll just make things worse if he gets wind of this. Barook needs to stay by Rodney's side to offer comfort and advice. Make yourself available to Barook and the boy if and when they need you. And I will make myself available to you for any questions you might have. Be sure and let me know if any further complications arise."

"Thank you, Gabriel." Adoram was sure there would be no further complications, but then, he was an optimistic angel. He made his way out of the palace, through the cottage garden, then back down the golden streets. He flew back along the crystal wall which surrounded the city, and past its gates made of different gemstones. Before he got to his particular portal, Adoram passed by the HeavenLink that led to the dark side of the moon. It wasn't used very often. Adoram shuddered slightly, then shook his wings as if to clear himself of a bad feeling. Shortly thereafter he crossed dimensions for the third time in less than an hour.

Chapter 2

Oh, the depth of the riches
both of the wisdom and knowledge of God!
How unsearchable are His judgements,
and His ways past finding out.

~ Romans 11:33

Dominion angel Clovis and his elderly charge, Mrs. Snipperblister, were wandering through the rummage sale at The Church on the Way after the service had ended. Clovis had his guardian-angel hands full with this little spitfire. She came to church every Sunday and Wednesday, mostly out of boredom.

She didn't realize it, but Mrs. Snipperblister took great pleasure in making people feel guilty about things—things they were doing, things they were not doing, things they didn't do well enough. She told herself she was helping them to be better people, but in actuality she just enjoyed the nitpicking. There was usually a mischievous demonic power clinging to her back or sitting on her shoulder, prompting her to cut people down with an acerbic remark, or to wither them with her judgmental stare.

Today that demonic power was in the form of a furry little capuchin monkey with a brown muzzle. The little old lady picked up a Hummel, a painted porcelain figurine of two children dressed in old-fashioned country German clothing, huddling under an umbrella. "Oh, Stormy Weather," she squealed in delight.

Just then, Adoram whooshed in the door of the church classroom where the rummage sale was being held. He found Barook trying to be inconspicuous behind a rack of women's clothing. "Praise be to God! You have returned," whispered the guardian angel.

"Yes, I told Gabriel of the situation and he cleared me to help. I'll break the news to our boy over there. You stay here until I call for you," the seraph instructed. He made his way past some old, beat-up toys to a section of the room where Rodney was now arranging dusty DVDs on a shelf. After catching his breath for a few minutes, Rodney had continued with his duties.

"I can't believe you didn't see my amazing wipe-out," he was shouting to Kirby who was on the other side of the room. "I flew so high in the air I think I hit the ceiling. Luckily, I landed in a pile of clothes. Kim and Elias are going to be so mad they missed it."

"Uh huh," Kirby muttered noncommittally while looking down at his phone.

"Excuse me," said Adoram, spreading wide his glorious feathery white wings which quivered with the power of heaven.

The words "Oh wow!" fell out of Rodney's mouth as he turned and faced the angel. Then he tripped over a CD rack and face-planted on the floor, his strawberry-blond curls covering his face. Barook, peering from behind the rack of dresses, cringed. "Zounds! A fall and I've been remiss! I must get close if this wight is not to pierce himself through."

Mrs. Snipperblister, meanwhile, had picked up a second Hummel figurine of a child with small wings kneeling on a cloud. Her guardian angel Clovis looked over her shoulder and said, "Baby angels—how ridiculous! We don't look like that. After 20 years of listening to sermons, you know the truth. We aren't children." The capuchin screeched, scratched his bottom, and said into the old lady's ear, "Take it! Take it! You need that Hummel to complete your collection!" The septuagenarian deftly slid the figurine into her purse while furtively looking around her.

"What the what?" shouted Clovis.

Rodney lifted his head up off the floor and looked over at all the spirit-based commotion. "Is that a monkey?"

The white-haired woman looked around the room. "What monkey? Boy, are you daft?"

"Ahem." Adoram cleared his throat to get Rodney's attention back. "Young man, I have something very important to tell you."

Rodney stood up and swiveled his head back toward the glowing heavenly being. "I don't feel so well," Rodney mumbled. "I hit my head. I think I need a doctor. I should call 911." Rodney pulled his phone out, dialed the emergency services number, and managed to blurt out, "I have a head injury."

Adoram came closer to explain to Rodney what was happening, but the angel's glory overwhelmed Rodney and he fainted. Instead of hitting the floor, he fell onto the pink velvet loveseat bedecked with purple ribbons. The floor would have been less humiliating for him. Adoram began to worry that Rodney would not have the strength of mind to deal with his newfound vision without going crazy.

"Hey! Who's running this dog and pony show?" yelled Mrs. Snipperblister, looking around the room for someone to help her reach another Hummel high on a shelf. Clovis ran his hands over his face and sighed.

"I'll help you, ma'am," said Kirby ambling slowly in her direction.

♫♫♫♫

An ambulance raced along Sherman Way in Van Nuys and pulled up in front of The Church on the Way. Two EMTs hopped out of the front seats and quickly made their way to the back of the medical bus. They whipped open the back doors and pulled out a stretcher, its wheels dropping to meet the pavement as it emerged. Churchgoers were milling about like ants in sugar. One of the EMTs addressed a bystander in a suit, "We got a call about a head injury. Do you know where the guy is?" The churchgoer looked surprised. "Really? I have no idea. Let me find an elder for you." The suited man ducked into the nearest building to seek a church official. Next to the doorway was posted a flyer:

Church Bazaar Today!

Once inside the room, the churchgoer spied an old lady looking down at a pink velvet loveseat and yelling, "What in tarnation is wrong with you, boy? Are you asleep? Get up!" It took the interested bystander only two seconds to determine that Rodney was probably the head-injury in question. He called the EMTs over.

"Son? Can you hear me?" the emergency medical tech asked Rodney while pulling open the young man's eyelids. He shone a small flashlight into Rodney's green eyes to check whether or not the pupils dilated in reaction to the light.

"Wha? Huh? Who?" mumbled Rodney, coming back to consciousness after his fainting spell. "I, uh, hit my head. A couple of times actually," Rodney managed.

"He's really clumsy, that kid," Mrs. Snipperblister snorted. "I'll get his parents so they can spank him." Kirby pointed and chimed in, "I think they're over there."

Mr. and Mrs. Simplessohn reached the ambulance just as Rodney was being loaded inside. "Oh honey! What happened this time?" Sheryl Simplessohn asked, her forehead creasing with worry. A glowing female angel dressed in a full-length white linen tunic leaned toward her and whispered, "He'll be fine. God will protect him." Another glowing angel stood behind Mr. Simplessohn.

"Mom! Dad!" Rodney was genuinely glad to see their familiar, comforting faces. Usually he felt like they were nosing around in his business too much, but at this moment, he was grateful they figured out what was happening. "I had this super-wicked accident with a trampoline. You should have seen it. I hit the ceiling and then the floor. I wish someone had caught it on video. And now I'm seeing things—weird things, freaky things. So, these dudes want to take me to the hospital to get checked out. They think I have a concussion. Dad, who's your friend? And why is he wearing a white dress? Is there a play going on later today at church? What's the deal with all the costumes?"

Sheryl looked around and then over at her husband, David, and frowned. There was no man in a dress, white or otherwise, near them. She began to fear for her son's sanity. She ran to the front of the ambulance and told the driver to take her son to Providence St. Joseph in Burbank. "I work in the brain imaging center. I'll follow you there."

Rodney stared at the closed ambulance doors from his stretcher inside the bus. Suddenly he saw a radiant heavenly being with six wings fly through the doors and settle beside him.

"Rodney, you have been given the gift of spiritual sight. You have been allowed to see me, a seraph angel and Barook, your dominion angel there," spoke Adoram just as Barook materialized through the ambulance's metal double doors. "For the Lord of Hosts has purposed it, and who will annul it? His hand is stretched out and who will turn it back? He alone spreads out the heavens, and treads on the waves of the sea. He made the Bear, Orion, and the Pleiades, and the constellations in the skies to the south. He does great things past finding out, yes, wonders without number!"

"Wow, this hallucination is soooo real," Rodney muttered to himself. "Those wings are so detailed. The feathers are even shimmering. It's blowing my mind."

"O man, greatly beloved, fear not! Peace be to you. Be strong, yes, be strong. For the Lord will go before you, and the God of Israel will be your rear guard," Adoram continued. Just then the EMT assigned to the back opened the door and jumped in. "Off we go, kid. You're gonna be just fine."

"I'm having some excellent hallucinations right now. I wish you could see them," gushed Rodney. "There's this super-chill angel guy with six wings."

"Six wings" the EMT repeated, letting out a low whistle.

"Yeah. It's awesome. He's saying all sorts of Biblical-sounding stuff. And there's this other dude with two wings who mostly just stares at me with a weird look on his face. It's really funny."

Adoram looked at Barook and said, "This just might take some time."

∬∬

The ambulance pulled into the emergency entrance of St. Joseph's Medical Center in Burbank, California. The driver got out of the truck and walked around to the back. He opened the double doors letting the second EMT jump out of the back. Together they removed a stretcher topped by a goofy looking teenager with a curly mop of strawberry-blonde hair and lanky limbs. He looked dazed and confused. His eyes were darting all around like he was watching things that weren't really there. The EMTs wheeled him in to the emergency corridor of the hospital. It smelled faintly of hand sanitizer.

"Okay, kid," one EMT began explaining, "you're acting pretty funny so we're recommending an MRI. But you don't have a gunshot wound or anything, so we're going to transfer you to this wheelchair where you can wait for a few minutes while we give your paperwork to the intake nurse and your parents fill out the insurance forms. Can you walk?"

"Of course I can!" Rodney announced confidently as he slipped off the stretcher and onto the floor, his knees buckling underneath him. "Hashtag epic fail," he weakly mumbled from the ground.

The EMTs hauled him up and into the wheelchair. "We'll be right back," one of them said as they both disappeared around the corner of the corridor. Two nuns holding rosaries and praying were walking down the hallway towards Rodney. Cherubim angels circled in flight above the habited women's heads.

As the nuns moved closer, Rodney could hear their prayers. "And dear Lord, we pray that Christopher Smith has the power to break his addiction. Please send your angels to watch over him and help him fight against the demons of alcoholism and drug abuse." Rodney's mouth dropped open as one of the cherubim flapped his four wings and raised his flaming sword to heaven. The cherub nodded in acknowledgement of his assignment and flew up through the ceiling in a flash of lightning. The nuns couldn't see any of this, but Rodney could.

"Holy moly!" Rodney whispered. "That is so real. Unbelievable."

"Believe it!" announced Adoram from Rodney's side with Barook in tow.

"Oh! You two again," Rodney moaned. "This just won't end! What is going on?"

"It's called *geisterseherkraft*. You're seeing something few people ever have the privilege of witnessing. You're seeing angels in action to protect humans against the attacks of demons which happen every day. You're seeing how humans have the power to sway the battle by calling in angelic help. And soon, you'll see the whole range of demonic beings trying to overwhelm people's souls, in order to keep them from finding and knowing God."

"No, no, no, no, no, no. That can't be right. That doesn't make any sense. I haven't heard of any of this stuff," insisted Rodney.

"Are you sure about that? Wasn't your preacher talking about the battle against spiritual hosts of wickedness just this morning?"

"Oh, that. Sure, yeah. I've heard that. But nobody really takes that stuff literally. I mean, c'mon. It's all just symbolic, right?" Just then another cherub wielding a flaming sword whooshed past Rodney's head. Adoram and Barook both gave him a knowing look.

"I think I'm gonna be sick," Rodney said pathetically.

∫∫∫∫

Rodney finally rolled into the imaging center of St. Joseph's where he waited his turn for the MRI machine. The emergency room doctor who examined him wanted to see if there were signs of a brain injury from bleeding or swelling. The room was familiar to him because his mother worked here. But he had never actually gotten an MRI before. Rodney looked around the waiting room at the people gathered there. He saw an elderly black woman with her eyes closed and her hands folded in prayer. Rodney saw two scorpions crawling on her head. They had a dark yet glowing quality to them. Adoram pointed to her and told Rodney, "God wants to heal her."

"So, God should do that. He should also tell her about those scorpions."

"Those demon scorpions signify sickness. He will take care of them, but He wants to work through you."

"Why?"

"So that His name may be glorified and her faith increased."

"Well, what does that have to do with me?"

"God wants you to tell her that good news."

"She'll think I'm crazy," said Rodney shaking his red head.

"She already thinks that," replied Adoram nodding his head at the woman who was now staring at Rodney with a worried look on her face. "You are talking to an empty space in front of you."

"I don't wanna," said Rodney turning his head down and to the side so he couldn't see Adoram any longer. "I can't adult right now."

"God will never force you," the angel replied, dropping the subject.

∫∫∫∫

After the magnetic resonance image was taken of his head, Rodney was brought into Dr. Hagopian's office where his mother was waiting. Sheryl had followed Rodney's progress through the hospital emergency room to here, aided by her connections with her co-workers. She had just gotten the scoop from Dr. Hagopian on Rodney's MRI. Rodney recognized the doctor from previous visits to his mother's office.

"Oh, hey man," Rodney weakly managed to say, afraid of what he might hear.

"Good news, young man," said Dr. Hagopian. "Your skull is rock hard. And even though your brain is as soft as butter, it seems to have emerged unharmed from your recent adventures. But, I'm keeping you here overnight for observation, just in case anything changes. Your mother mentioned that you might be having hallucinations."

"Yeah. I might be," answered Rodney while casting his eyes down toward his shoes.

Chapter 3

The Lord God has given me the tongue of the learned, that I should know how to speak a word in season to him who is weary.

~ Isaiah 50:4a

In the hospital bed next to Rodney's, a man in his 40's was lying down, his face contorted in pain, his knee in a sling. As the nurses were transferring Rodney from his gurney to his bed, he saw dragon-shaped demons shooting sharp quills from their tails into the middle-aged man's knee. A woman with long blond hair laid her hands over his wounded knee and began to pray out loud, "Dear Lord, please send your angels to protect Jim."

A winged cherub swooped into the room and folded his wings over the sick man. The poisoned darts and arrows thudded into the angel's wings instead of into their fleshy target. "And please, Father God, protect his torn ligaments from further injury." The cherub lifted his flaming sword, pointed it at one of the demon dragons, and fired a bolt of lightning that swept the evil spirit out of the room. The second demon, with fear on his face, flew out voluntarily.

Rodney's eyes, full of the import of what they had just taken in, were about to pop out of his head. Right then, the blond woman looked up at Rodney and saw his distress. She apologized and drew the curtain between the two beds.

Shortly thereafter, a Korean-American boy called Kim walked in followed by his dominion angel. Wearing the white linen uniform of every guardian angel, Koram greeted his old pal Barook, and Adoram who was also Koram's supervising angel. As the angels conversed about Rodney and *geisterseherkraft*, the boys carried on in their usual manner.

"Suh, bro!" said Kim as he looked his best friend over.

"Hey, ham bone!" Rodney practically shouted back. You must have ridden your bike here. No way your dad let you borrow the car on a Sunday afternoon."

"Yeah. I couldn't pass up the chance to make fun of you in person, bacon bits," said Kim.

Kim had been friends with the clumsy one for years. Their parents knew each other well and encouraged the youths to hang out together. Rodney's parents had always felt that they were getting the better part of that deal. Although they were the same age, Kim was more mature and grounded than Rodney. The Simplessohns knew he was a good influence on their somewhat silly son. Kim pulled out his phone and held it up in front of Rodney. "So, let's hear it in vivid detail."

"You're making an iMovie of this?"

"Of course I am. Walk me through all of the gloriously painful parts."

Rodney complied with his friend's request, recounting his trip on the bouncing fitness ball, then on top of the ball plus a skateboard, and from there to the mini trampoline which had an immense amount of springiness for its size. He described flying through the air, feeling a little weird and elated near the ceiling, and then falling back toward the ground without being afraid for some inexplicable reason. Then Rodney told how he landed in a soft pile of clothes without injury.

"So what are you doing in here?"

"Well, after that I tripped and smashed my face into the floor. That really hurt."

"So falling from the ceiling left you unbruised, but landing on the floor from five feet away put you in the hospital?"

"Well, I think what really got me here was the fact that I .. . do we have to record this part?"

"Yes. Spill the tea."

"I kind of fainted. I know—epic fail on my part."

Kim burst into laughter, his hand shaking so much he could barely keep Rodney in frame. "Oh man, I'm dead."

"I hope you win an Oscar. Now can you put that away? I have something serious to ask you."

"K. That's comedy gold right there. I think I have enough." Kim pocketed his phone and sat down in a chair next to Rodney's hospital bed. "What's on your mind? Are you worried about whether or not the nurse saw your butt? Because she probably did. Or maybe you're nervous that the person next to you over there is also laughing at you?" Kim peeked around the curtain. "Nope. He's asleep."

"Do you believe in angels and demons?"

"Wait, what? I wasn't prepared for that question," stammered Kim. "Where did that come from? Did the doctors say anything about you having a head injury?"

"Well, they said I don't have one, but they are keeping me here overnight just to make sure that's true. I want to know what you think about angels with wings and glowing bodies and flaming swords." Rodney stole a glance over at Koram, Barook, and Adoram who were now suddenly listening to the teenagers' conversation.

"Like what Pastor Temple preached on today?" asked Kim.

"Yeah. Is that stuff real? Or it just symbolic?" asked Rodney. "Are we supposed to take it literally?"

"I think so. Why?"

"Well," Rodney formed the words slowly, not wanting to tip his hand just yet, "I mean if those things were real, wouldn't we be hearing stories about heavenly spirits all the time? If they're with us, all around us, wouldn't people be picking up on it?"

"I guess you could say that's what miracles are—evidence of the spiritual realm crossing into our reality."

"K, but shouldn't there be more YouTube videos about it?"

"Have you looked?"

"No."

"Let's see, then." Kim pulled up YouTube on his phone's browser and both boys leaned over to take a look.

They found a music video of the Alabama song "Angels Among Us," and a review of Frank Peretti's book *This Present Darkness* by a goofy kid named Jose Taco Cruz. They also found a painting called "Spiritual Warfare" by Ron DiCianni. It showed a man praying over his young son. It was captioned, "The effectual fervent prayer of a righteous man availeth much ~James 5:16."

"I guess I'm talking about real-life interactions and experiences, not songs or books or paintings," said Rodney. "But I suppose it would be like getting an alien on video. It's just not that likely to happen."

"No, it isn't." Kim shook his head and put his phone down. "Does that change your belief in them?"

"What if I told you I saw one?" asked Rodney timidly.

"Saw one what?" asked Kim, his eyes widening. "An angel or a demon?"

"Well, two of them, actually. Angels. Two angels. I saw two angels in the ambulance on the way over here."

"Whoa. That's lit. I mean, it sounds lit. Was it lit?"

"Um, yeah. It's amazing. One of them has six wings. The other one has two wings, and he is glowing with this yellow-brown color that looks like the ring my mom wears sometimes. I think she calls it topaz. They're both kind of glowing like topaz. They're wearing these white linen dress-like outfits that people in Bible times wore. The six-winged one has a golden sash like a beauty queen's."

"Why did you say they 'are glowing' instead of they 'were glowing'?" Kim's eyes narrowed a bit as he asked the question.

"Because they are glowing. I'm looking at them right now." Rodney focused his eyes on the three now very quiet angels in the corner of the room.

"Holy mother of God," whispered Kim, looking around the room trying to follow Rodney's gaze. "Where?"

"In the corner over there." Rodney pointed to Barook who smiled weakly and then to Adoram who gave a slight wave of his hand. Kim couldn't make out a thing.

"Give me your phone," said Rodney. "I'll take a picture of them."

When the boys looked at the photo Rodney had taken, all that showed up was an empty corner of a hospital room.

"I don't see anything. How come I can't see them? Are you sure this isn't your head injury giving you weird visions?" asked Kim.

"I'm not sure, actually. I could be going crazy. But your guardian angel, the one who came in with you, is waving at me right now."

"Well, if he's my guardian angel, then he should know something about me that you couldn't possibly know, right?"

"I guess so."

"So, ask him to tell you something that you wouldn't know otherwise. You can hear them, right?"

"Yes, I can hear them. It's really freaking me out, bro. I don't know if I can quite handle this. Wait, your guy just said that you stubbed your toe this morning before church. And that you cursed when it happened! Oh, snap!"

"Well," said Kim, his face reddening, "I guess it's not a hallucination after all."

Rodney got out of his bed and wandered over to the angels, waving his hands and arms in front of him. He couldn't feel anything as his hands passed through their spirit bodies. "Well, I for sure can't feel them," he told Kim as he climbed back into his bed, being careful to keep the back of his hospital gown closed.

"K. What if they are a vision? Like in the Bible?" asked Kim.

"That's bad."

"Maybe not. Maybe that's a good thing. I mean, it shows that there really is more to life than we can see. Haven't we been wanting some kind of proof of that? Haven't we both questioned what life is all about? Maybe this is the meaning we've been searching for. Maybe you've finally found your destiny. You're always saying you don't have a purpose or know what it is. Maybe this is your purpose."

"You're making my head hurt. I'm not ready for this," Rodney whined.

"I don't think God waits until we're ready," Kim said as he wandered into the area that Rodney had pointed to a few seconds ago. "Are they over here?" Kim began waving his hands around and through the angels without seeing them. He continued his speech, "David wasn't ready to be anointed as king when the prophet Samuel sought him out. Abraham wasn't expecting to have a baby when he was an old man and the angels visited him. Joseph didn't ask to be made ruler of Egypt. Stuff just happened to them and they dealt with it. If they can do it, you can, too."

The angel Koram smiled proudly at his charge's good advice. "What does my angel look like?" asked Kim, whipping his head around to try to catch a glimpse of the angelic being assigned to him.

"What if my faith isn't strong enough?" asked Rodney, ignoring Kim's last question.

"I don't think it has anything to do with you. I think it has everything to do with Jesus and his work on the cross. Jesus did it all for us. All we have to do is rely on Him. Look to Him. He's already conquered death and hell, remember? He'll get you through this."

"That's some real talk, dude," said Rodney feeling comforted by his friend's words. "If these are really angels, I wonder what they want with me," he wondered aloud.

∫∫∫∫

The next morning, Rodney's mom stopped by her son's hospital room on her way to work in the imaging center. "Dad sends his love," she said while sitting herself down on the edge of Rodney's bed.

Rodney groaned awake and turned to face his mother. "Dad and you were just here last night. This is no big deal, Mom." He hadn't told his mom about his *geisterseherkraft* last night and he was wondering whether he should break the news to her this morning.

"I know, honey. But we're your parents. It's our job to worry over you, so get used to it."

Now was not the time to tell her about his newfound vision. Even Rodney was smart enough to pick up on that.

"K. Hey, Mom, do you ever feel like you should do a good deed, but then don't do it?"

"Well, yes, actually. All the time."

"Really?"

"Yeah. For instance, I should call your grandmother more often. And take more pictures of you. And bring our elderly neighbors dinner more often. You know, the Jacksons? They aren't in the best health and I know they appreciate it. I just get busy and let these things slide. I'm not proud of it."

"Well, I kinda had the feeling that God wanted me to say something to a lady in your waiting room yesterday. But I didn't do it. I didn't want her to think I was a nut."

"Oh honey, I understand that you're scared. But God has put a prompting in your heart."

"It's more like my face. He put it in my face."

"Okay, your face. He is giving you a chance to be a blessing. And I promise you, you will feel relieved if you follow through on it. What's a little embarrassment in light of that?"

"Well, when you put it that way, I feel like a jerk," Rodney mumbled while stuffing his face in his pillow.

His mom stroked his curly red hair. "I don't want you to feel bad. I want you to feel blessed and happy and at peace with yourself. I have to go to work now. Come see me before you leave. Dr. Hagopian will stop by in a little while to tell you when you can go home."

Rodney waved goodbye as she left the room. He threw the covers off and searched the room for any sight of angels or demons. He saw his guardian angel standing near the window.

"Barook, that's your name, right? Where is that other guy who's usually here with you, and where is the lady that you wanted me to talk to yesterday? Is she still here in the hospital? I think I'm ready to talk to her today."

"Huzzah! Pride is swelling within me. In point of fact, Adoram has gone back to our heavenly realm for the time being, and the dame you seek is breakfasting this morn in the public house on the first floor."

"You mean the cafeteria? We're gonna need to update your vocab. You're killing me with that old English." Barook nodded and then winced a little.

♫♫♫

Barook led Rodney downstairs to the cafeteria of Providence St. Joseph Hospital. Rodney gleefully inhaled the aroma of sizzling hash browns and sausage. At a table that Barook pointed toward, the elderly woman from the waiting room was eating scrambled eggs and reading *Time* magazine. She was supposed to have had an MRI yesterday afternoon to check on the size of her brain tumor, but a weird kid was brought in before her, and her appointment got pushed back. She decided not to wait after watching that crazy red-headed boy have a full conversation with the wall. She had better things to do. So, she re-scheduled for 9 a.m. today. After arriving early and checking in with the nice receptionist at the imaging center, she decided to grab a quick bite to eat. The food wasn't bad—for a cafeteria.

Barook, still stinging from Rodney's criticism of his vernacular, spoke to Rodney in the voice of a cage-match announcer, "Ladies and gentlemen, the devil's number one tactic—that's right number one—is to make you think you don't have what you already have! You heard me! But hear this: Blessed be the God and Father of our Lord Jesus Christ, who has blessed us with every spiritual blessing in the heavenly places in Christ. That's right! I said every spiritual blessing!"

Rodney rolled his eyes at Barook. "I'm not sure I like this announcer voice, either."

As he made his way over to Mrs. Washington's table, he noticed the scorpions of sickness were, in fact, gone. Without introducing himself, he blurted out, "God wants me to tell you that you are healed."

Mrs. Washington looked Rodney up and down. She recognized him from their previous encounter. "Look, I don't know who you are or why you are accosting me like this, but I don't feel healed, son. Not that it's any of your business," she retorted.

"Well you are. So there," Rodney sputtered. He shot a look at Barook who hung his head in shame and frustration. "I mean," Rodney started over. "God wants your faith to grow and He wants you to know that you are healed." Not knowing Mrs. Washington skipped yesterday's appointment, an idea hit him. "You should go back to the imaging center for another test. My mom works there. I'll explain to her why you need another scan. C'mon," he said excitedly as he reached for her arm.

Recoiling, Mrs. Washington glared at him and shot back, "Why should I go anywhere with you? You're obviously out of your ever-loving mind. Get away from me before I scream."

"Whoa! K," Rodney acquiesced and backed away. "Forget I said anything." On his way out of the room, he glared at Barook who was by his side. "Well, that went well."

Trying out the cadence and vocabulary of a 1940's gangster, Barook responded, "Ya weren't considering her feelings in this matter, see? Youz were thinking only of yourself. You're too ready to blow this joint, see?"

For a moment, Rodney forgot everything but how his angel was talking. "Look, if you're with me all the time, you must have seen some of the TV shows I watch, right? Can't you mimic the way people talk in those? We're living in the 20th century now." Remembering what just happened, he added, "And anyway, I did what you wanted. I'm officially off the hook. I don't care what happens now."

Barook looked both sad and a bit befuddled. He thought for a moment before saying in a very stilted accent, "Yo, that's rough bra. It cuts me that you feel that way. And we are, uh, living in the 21st century, by the way."

"K, don't use modern gangster rap either. That just sounds ridiculous coming out of you. Let's go see if Dr. Hagopian will let me go home now." Then, after a beat, "Really? The 21st century? Huh."

∫∫∫

Mrs. Washington made her way back to the imaging center for her appointment, a little shaken by her confrontation with Rodney. She walked up to Sheryl Simplessohn sitting at the reception desk. "Are you the lady with the crazy son?" she demanded.

Sheryl was nonplussed. "Probably. Red-headed, skinny, 18 years old?"

"Yeah, that's him. Fool said I was healed. I don't believe him, of course. But I guess we'll find out soon enough."

"Come on back. We're ready for you." Sheryl led her into the room with the MRI machine. After the scan was completed, Sheryl asked Mrs. Washington to wait in Dr. Hagopian's office for the results.

Dr. Hagopian sat down at his desk across from Mrs. Washington. "I have some incredible news for you. Now, it's possible that these results are erroneous, so I'm scheduling you to come back next week for a follow-up. But your brain scan shows perfect circulation in the damaged section here." He pointed to the MRI. "And I don't see any sign of that small tumor. Two weeks ago, you had the scan of a person with memory loss and mood swings. Today you have the scan of a person with a perfectly healthy brain. I don't understand it. I've never seen a recovery like this. It just doesn't happen—I don't care how much fish oil you were taking."

"Sweet Jesus!" exclaimed Mrs. Washington, pushing out of her chair and getting down on her knees. "I believe, Lord!" she yelled with her hands slapping the carpet in front of her. "I'm sorry I doubted it." Holding her hands together and looking up toward heaven, ignoring the doctor altogether she said, "I know how much You love me, Jesus, and I know how powerful You are. I claim this healing and I praise Your holy name."

"Yes, well, like I said," Dr. Hagopian continued, trying to politely ignore Mrs. Washington's dramatic outburst, "it's possible the machine is malfunctioning, so we'll do this again next week just to be sure."

"You could do it again every day for the rest of my life—you'll find the same thing!" Mrs. Washington yelled as Dr. Hagopian helped her up from the floor. "I have the perfect mind of Christ because He lives in me! Amen! Thank you, Jesus!" she exclaimed as she left his office. With a big smile on her face, she pointed to Sheryl on her way out and said, "Your boy was right! Hallelujah! Thank him for me. Thank him for being brave enough to try to bring good news to a stranger."

Sheryl raised her eyebrows, a look of astonishment on her face.

Chapter 4

Now acquaint yourself with Him and be at peace
so that good will come to you.
Receive, please, instruction from His mouth
and lay up His words in your heart.

~ Job 12:21-22

Rodney was riding home from the hospital in the back seat of a Lyft car. Barook, the dominion angel assigned to keep Rodney safe and on the right spiritual track, was flying just above the car. With his wings spread wide, Barook was bigger than the Prius below him. Barook's supervising angel, Adoram, was flying next to him. He was checking in on the pair, making sure Rodney didn't become unhinged by his newfound *geisterseherkraft*—a kind of spiritual perception that allowed him to see angels and demons everywhere he looked. Because Rodney didn't want anyone but Kim to know about his supernatural gift just yet, and because he didn't want to appear crazy in front of strangers, he had warned his angels that he would ignore them during the ride home.

Inside the car, the Lyft driver named Mike attempted a conversation. "So, are you feeling better? You said you were just released, right?"

"Oh yeah, I'm fine, thanks. Just like the doctor said, no permanent damage," answered Rodney. Then, under his breath, "Nothing that shows up on tests, anyway."

"Glad to hear it," said Mike. A little Pomeranian dog put his paws up on the back of the front seat, peered around, and gave Rodney what looked like a smile. Rodney laughed at how adorable this pup was with his tongue hanging out.

Rodney's eyes wandered out the window to the sidewalk as the car pulled up to a red light somewhere in the patchwork of streets along the flat desert floor of Los Angeles' San Fernando Valley. There he noticed a man in filthy clothes with matted hair rummaging through a trash can. Rodney could see an evil spirit shaped like an octopus gripping the man's chest and arms. He was beginning to recognize the glow of beings who weren't visible physically. Supernatural frogs hopped around the man's legs and on his head. "Oh yikes!" Rodney unintentionally blurted out at the sight of the evil principalities. The Pomeranian looked out the window and barked. Following their gazes, Mike said, "Not everyone has a pleasant way to make a living."

"I—I know. I didn't mean to be insensitive. I'm sorry." Just then one of the demon frogs jumped out of the trash can and onto the window of the car. "Ahhh!" screamed Rodney as he recoiled in surprise. The dog barked furiously at it. Realizing too late that Mike wouldn't be able to see the frog, Rodney began to make up an excuse for his being startled. "There are roaches in there. Oh, poor guy. I guess he's used to them by now. Oh, man." Rodney was beginning to suspect that the dog could see the demons. He wondered if animals could see angels as well.

The spirit frog, named Scumbert, was about to leap off the window when he noticed something: Rodney was looking back at him. Demons and angels clocked each other constantly, but this boy wasn't supposed to be able to see him. This boy even fell backwards a bit when he landed on the window. What was going on here? Scumbert decided to stay on the window as the car continued along. He decided he would investigate this situation further. Torturing the homeless man could wait.

The Prius pulled onto Hart Street, just east of Van Nuys airport, a not-so-charming but safe area that was affordable to those in the middle and upper-lower classes. Rodney usually enjoyed scanning the airport tarmac for fancy private jets owned by people who lived in Beverly Hills or Calabassas. He wasn't in the mood to do that right now. Mike eased his car into Rodney's driveway and Rodney jumped out, eager to get upstairs to his room—his sanctuary where he could mull things over, maybe figure some things out before he headed to school. As Rodney walked up his driveway, he noticed his Pacer was parked on the curb. He figured his mom and dad must have picked it up from the church's parking lot for him. He took two seconds to appreciate their efforts as he unlocked the front door.

Barook and Adoram landed and followed Rodney on foot, stepping in front of Scumbert as he hopped after the young man. Rodney's angel helpers were not comfortable with this frog following Rodney. They knew what was at stake if the demon found out about the boy's new powers. They had been instructed to keep it secret from the demon principalities for as long as possible. Adoram didn't want to tip the frog off by shooing it away. Maybe he should have risked it.

Rodney ran upstairs, into his room, closed his door, and leaned against it with a sigh. As he did so, his companion angels floated through the door and flew into the center of the room, followed by Scumbert whose eyes were glowing red. Adoram wanted to warn Rodney not to reveal his special sight to the demon frog. But how to warn Rodney without talking to him? And how to tell Rodney not to talk to them? Just then, the family's cat wandered up the stairs and, seeing Rodney's door closed, tried turning the doorknob with her paws. Rodney, startled by the noise and the movement of the doorknob, jumped away from the door and stared at it. Miss Kitty managed on a second try to get the door ajar. She pushed it open with her sleek black furry body and slinked into the room. "Mra!" she demanded.

This gave Adoram an idea. Maybe he could tip off Rodney while pretending to talk to the cat. "I wonder if Rodney senses the presence of a principality" he said a bit too loudly while staring at Scumbert.

"Yes, Adoram, I sense its presence" said Rodney, looking at the frog who was hopping around Rodney's dirty socks and underwear scattered all over the floor. So much for that plan.

Rodney then switched his gaze to the cat. "Hey guys, tell me about Miss Kitty. I can see that she is looking at you. Can animals see spirits?"

Barook was waving his hands excitedly back and forth while shaking his head "no." The bullfrog was now studying Rodney, taking note of the fact that he answered a question he shouldn't have been able to hear, and was seeing things that he shouldn't be able to see. Barook threw his hands over Rodney's mouth and allowed them to materialize for a moment. He was attempting to prevent further damage, but the jig was up. Scumbert was onto them.

"Whab arb you booing?" Rodney asked Barook through muffled lips. Scumbert let out an excited "Ribbet, ribbet, ribbet!" and hopped out the second-floor window onto a nearby tree. Scumbert didn't want to start a confrontation. He was in over his head in this situation. He decided he would hang out in the tree and watch for a bit, unseen if possible. He needed more information before he could comfortably report anything.

Adoram watched him go and declared, "Well that didn't take long. So much for keeping things under wraps for a few days."

"Whab nowb?" asked Rodney. Barook took his hands off the boy's mouth, dematerialized them, and said, "I thank you Father, Lord of heaven and earth, that you have hidden these things from the wise but revealed them to babes."

"But why me?" whined Rodney. "What did I do to deserve this? I'm no Bible hero. I'm not very devout. I don't pray all the time or study the scriptures. I didn't ask for gastric ulcers or whatever it's called."

Adoram answered him, "Blessed are the eyes which see the things you see, for I tell you that many prophets and kings have desired to see what you see, and have not seen it, and to hear what you hear, and have not heard it."

"But I didn't desire to see them or hear them. I don't understand," said Rodney rolling his eyes back in his head and flopping backwards onto his bed. "I'm gonna text mom. I don't feel well enough to go to school today. I'm a hot mess right now. I'll go tomorrow."

Barook knelt down beside Rodney's bed and said quietly, "That sounds like a good plan. It will give us time to pray and think. Hopefully that will make you feel better."

"K," said Rodney closing his eyes and clasping his hands together on top of his chest. "Good idea. What did you say your name was again?"

"Barook."

"I'll call you Bazooka."

"Let's pray." Barook raised his hands to heaven and recited, "Show me your ways, O Lord; teach me your paths. Lead me in your truth and teach me, for you are the God of my salvation. On you I wait all the day long."

"Amen," said Rodney. "Thanks for talking like a normal person, Bazooka. So, did the prayer work?"

"Let's go now to the source to find all knowledge and the answer to this question."

"The source of all knowledge? What's that? A sphinx or something?"

"No, it's a book stuffed full with grace for those who look. God wrote His wisdom in it; pick it up and find no limit."

"You're sounding a little weird again. I think you mean the Bible. I have one right here. I don't read it very much. It confuses me."

"Turn to Psalm 32:8."

"Psalm, Psalm, Psalm," mumbled Rodney flipping through the clean pages of his pristine Bible looking for the old testament book of songs written by King David. "Where is that? After John?"

"You have a lot of work to do," sighed Adoram, looking sympathetically at Barook. The family cat meowed in agreement. To the cat, Adoram said, "Keep an eye on that demon frog. Don't let him get too close to Rodney." To Rodney and Barook he said, "I must be getting back to heaven now."

Barook nodded as he and Rodney watched Adoram flap his beautiful, shimmering angel wings and fly out the window.

∫∫∫∫

The frog-shaped principality, Scumbert, was still in the tree outside Rodney's window when Adoram flew out. Something clicked inside Scumbert's devilish mind. He figured seraph angels wouldn't hang around earth unless something important was going on. His brain wasn't huge, but it was big enough to figure out that he should report this up the food chain. He was naïve enough to think this would earn him a reward.

Scumbert hopped out of the tree, across Rodney's lawn, and into the gutter. He then bounced his way down an alley and into a trash dumpster. He planned to wait there for the garbage truck to make its early evening pickup. Then he would hitch a ride in the truck to the city dump without expending too much energy. Angels and demons could move through air and matter much more easily than humans, but it still took a bit of their energy to get from one place to another. In order to hitch a ride on a vehicle in this dimension, Scumbert would have to materialize just enough to be pulled along by it. He enjoyed the sensation. Demons did it all the time. Angels could do it, too, but they usually preferred flying.

∫∫∫∫

"Oh, I found it—the book of Psalms. It's in the Old Testament," Rodney declared to his guardian angel, Barook.

"Well done, Rodney," Barook condescended.

"What was the verse you wanted me to find again?"

"Chapter 32, verse 8."

"Oh yeah. Here it is: 'I will instruct you and teach you in the way you should go; I will guide you with My eye.' Well, that's comforting," admitted Rodney.

"Yes, it's meant to be. The Word is power. Through it you are put together and shaped up for the tasks God has for you. The Word gives light, gives understanding to the simple, to you."

"Hey! Are you calling me stupid?" teased Rodney.

"An empty-headed man will be wise when a wild donkey's colt is born a man," winked Barook, quoting a very old saying.

"I don't know what that means, but I'm pretty sure I should be offended," laughed the young man.

After a few more hours of looking up verses with Barook which included many, many minutes of taking breaks, snacking, watching some videos, and otherwise dawdling, Rodney heard his mom call out from the bottom of the stairs, "Dinner in ten minutes!"

"Great!" Rodney yelled back, jumping up from the bed and running downstairs with relish.

"What are we having?" he asked as he reached the kitchen, looking over his mother's shoulder to the stove.

"Your favorite: pasta shells stuffed with a blend of spinach and ricotta cheese."

"With your marinara sauce?" demanded Rodney lifting the lid off a stock pot to see for himself.

"Naturally."

"And are you baking it in the oven under a blanket of mozzarella?" he inquired, flipping on the oven light to take a peek.

"Of course. Now set the table," she said, pleased her son was acting like his usual, food-loving self.

"How are you feeling, son?" asked David Simplessohn as Rodney was pulling placemats out of the sideboard in the dining room.

"I'm alright, Dad."

"I always knew that knucklehead of yours was as hard as a rock."

"Yeah, well. . ." trailed off Rodney as he noticed for the first time that a glowing lady angel was following his mother around while a topaz-colored male angel shadowed his father.

Barook followed Rodney's gaze and introduced Sheba and Nimrod, the Simplessohns' guardian angels. They both waved hello to Rodney.

"Yep, the Simplessohns are tough, son. We take a licking and keep on ticking!" David said as he slammed his fist on the dining room table.

Rodney just rolled his eyes while Nimrod broke up laughing. Rodney stared at Nimrod in amazement. He couldn't believe that anyone found his dad funny, much less a higher being from another dimension. That made no sense.

Rodney's mom yelled from the kitchen "Hey Rodney, tell your dad about your mission from God in the hospital. And then I will update you both on the outcome."

"There's an outcome? Is it a good one?" asked Rodney incredulously.

"Oh, yeah. It's a good one. David, come here and get the garlic bread."

As David wandered back into the kitchen to collect the bread from his wife, Rodney whispered to the spirits, "Listen. You guys are super distracting. I don't want to look insane in front of my parents. At least not tonight, anyway. So, can you all just lay low during dinner? Please?"

♫♫♫

Scumbert hopped out of the garbage truck as it was depositing its payload onto a trash mountain inside Sun Valley's solid waste landfill. It took him a few minutes to hop over to the large building housing the incinerator, where one of the L.A. portals to hell was located. There were other portals: in sales offices of car dealerships, politicians' waiting rooms, and one in a law school. Scumbert bounced through the flames and emerged on the other side of the portal into a fiery cave. Sulfurous gas was everywhere. A red-orange glow from several small fires tinted the clouds of gas so that the cave looked like the stage of an Imagine Dragons concert. Scumbert spied what he was looking for: a red velvet rope restraining a crowd.

A huge, ape-like demon played the part of bouncer, letting only beautiful women past him through the red door. The men would have to wait. Scumbert hopped up to the bouncer who held up a black, leathery hand and said, "Whoa pal. Where do you think you're going? Do you have an appointment?"

"No, but I saw something that the Prince of Darkness is going to want to know about."

"Let me call my supervisor."

"It's—croak—rather urgent."

"There are protocols in place. Wait here."

The ape-shaped evil power guarding the entrance to hell's hottest nightclub spoke into his headset and then went back to monitoring the crowd. About 20 minutes later he told the frog, "The god of this world will see you now."

"It's about—ribbit—time," muttered the demon frog who had a powerful secret to share. He hopped in through the red door and was ushered by a demon goat through a dance floor packed with beautiful people wearing sexy Kardashian Kollection outfits designed to provoke lustful thoughts. For the most part, they were fulfilling their purpose. Scumbert attempted not to be skewered by shiny Louboutin heels as he hoppingly wove through the gyrating bodies toward another door marked "VIP."

This room was a bit quieter. Music was playing but it wasn't ear-meltingly loud. The walls appeared to be a blend of rock and metal, shiny swirls of reflective silver threaded through obsidian-black granite. In one corner, a backlit bar was stocked with fine liqueurs and aged scotch. Young, pouty women lounged on red leather couches and eyed each other suspiciously.

"Have you gained weight?" an ingénue in a black mini dress asked a skinny girl wearing a sequined top and spandex shorts.

"What? No! Have you gotten stupider?"

One entire wall was taken up by a bank of video screens showing live satellite feeds from various places on earth. One monitor displayed a Chinese factory worker mixing lead into a large vat of lipstick. Another showed an image of people in India dumping pots of dirty water into the Ganges. Next to that a screen showed a Belgian man driving like a maniac on a multi-lane motorway. Below that image, the frog saw an American banker in his office saying, "It's worth the risk. We stand to gain millions, if not billions." And next to that, a screen showed a kid screaming at his parents, "I don't have to listen to you!" In the bottom right corner monitor, a scientist was saying to his lab-mate, "God is a construct imagined by man. So is Satan for that matter. There is no such thing as a horned man with goat-feet clutching a pitchfork." At that, the demon bullfrog turned his bulging round eyes toward Satan and saw a cherub angel with a scowl on his face and a black silk suit tailored to fit around his four wings. His feet were mounted on wheels within wheels that let him glide along like he was perpetually riding a Segway. He was sipping a shot of 100-year-old Scotch. Lucifer looked down as the frog approached.

"Yes? What is it? I hear you have something important to tell me."

"Well, sir—croooaaaaak—it's just a little thing, but you always tell us that little things lead to big things."

"Quite right. Go on."

"I saw a person in L.A. who can see the spiritual realm."

"Another person with *geisterseherkraft*? Well that's not such a big deal. Just engage him in conversation in public a few times. The police will arrest him. Taunt him in the station and they'll send him to the psych ward. Done! It's standard procedure. You bothered me for this?"

"Well, it's more complicated than that, Your Foulness. This young man is a Christian. He had two angels around him: his dominion angel and another one that outranked you. That one had six wings and a golden sash."

"A seraph? A seraph angel was with him?"

"Ribbit!"

"Did you happen to catch this angel's name?"

"Adorable or something—croooaaak."

"Not Adoram?"

"Yes—craaaacket. That's it!"

"Adoram, eh? There's a blast from the past." Satan's eyes drifted upwards as he swirled his Scotch. "Do you know the young man's address by any chance?"

"Ribbit!"

"Good. You can leave now. Send Tricklane in on your way out. He's right outside the door."

Scumbert hesitated a bit. "I thought this information might, croak, be worth something to you."

"Oh, did you now?"

"Ribbit!"

Satan leaned down slowly until his face was near the frog's. In a quiet, menacing voice, he answered, "And I thought my underlings would lay down their lives for me."

Scumbert hopped away disappointed. He landed on the foot of a demon by the door who looked very much like a man in a dark, pin-striped suit. "He wants you," Scumbert croaked before he hopped off.

"I'm here my liege," the once-dominion angel announced as he entered the room.

"I need you to pull an address up on the monitors. It's in Los Angeles."

"Oh, I adore Los Angeles," Tricklane cooed as he typed the information into the EarthLink interface, "all that pollution, heavy traffic, disappointed and frustrated souls searching for answers from psychics and crystals. It's one of my favorite cities. Anyone can be convinced to sin spectacularly there. It's almost as good as Las Vegas."

"Yes, well, you might be paying your favorite city a visit soon. I need you to learn all you can about a young man who lives here. We need to destroy his faith, or his life—whichever is easier."

After a few seconds of typing, Tricklane said, "Here it is my lord." Up on the screen came an image of Rodney at the dinner table sitting between his mother and father. They were all holding hands. Hiding behind the dining room drapes, were Barook, Mr. Simplessohn's angel Nimrod, and Mrs. Simplessohn's angel Sheba. Plates were piled high with stuffed pasta shells, salad, and garlic bread. In unison, the three people and three angels were singing their mealtime prayer, "Praise God from whom all blessings flow; praise Him all creatures here below. Praise Him above ye heavenly host; praise Father, Son, and Holy Ghost."

"Turn it off!" screeched Satan, covering his ears with his hands. "Turn it off!"

Tricklane immediately shut down the connection and the screen went black. "I'm so sorry, your filthiness. I didn't know they would do that. Are you alright?"

"Oh, that sound. It pierces my flesh. It burns my ears."

"I'm so sorry. I didn't anticipate that they might be praising God."

"Be more careful next time!"

"Yes, your nastiness. I will."

"Go ahead and take that trip to the city of fallen angels for your recon mission. Take that stupid frog with you. I must go to the city of disgustingly *un*-fallen angels to do some business of my own. It won't be pleasant, but I don't see a way around it. We will meet again after I return."

Chapter 5

Watch and pray lest you enter into temptation.
The spirit indeed is willing, but the flesh is weak.

~ Matthew 26:41

Tricklane, one of Satan's cleverest helpers, was standing outside a house on Stone Canyon Road in Bel-Air, a swanky community built high on the hills south of the San Fernando Valley, just northwest of Beverly Hills. The fallen angel was talking to Scumbert, a frog demon who knew about Rodney Simplessohn and his power to see the spiritual realm. It was nighttime in Los Angeles. The sun had set spectacularly over the Pacific in a haze of pink and grey smog. Tricklane and Scumbert could see the silhouette of a beautiful actress in her 20s walking through her well-lit kitchen. Demon snakes slithered along her countertops.

"She's one of my most recent success stories, Scumbert. She used to be passionate about God when I first learned of her existence. Even though she ate ramen noodles every night for dinner in her shabby North Hollywood apartment, she still shared what little she had with anyone in need. Now look at her."

"How did she—ribbit—get so successful? Godliness doesn't always lead to this sort of life."

"All of this success, money, and fame was my gift to her. Now she has her own macrobiotic chef, washes her hair with Evian water, and holds onto every last cent. She's so busy working, she never has the time or energy to help anyone. She feels completely condemned by that fact, thanks to me. And instead of remembering how much God loves her, she's obsessed with her hair, her face, and which expensive car she should be seen driving. It's wonderful."

"Oh—craaaakik! You golden-handcuffed her, didn't you?"

"Yes. Nothing turns compassionate givers into selfish jerks faster than a huge income and a wallop of guilt. It works every time."

"You're very—ribbit—wise, sir. Rodney's house is on the other side of this hill and up that avenue."

"Let's proceed, then."

Soon the two demonic beings were standing outside the Simplessohn's house on a modest street in the San Fernando Valley. "Well, he's not rich. We might be able to use that," Tricklane was saying to his frog-shaped sidekick. Scumbert hopped up into the branches of a large tree and croaked out, "You can see into his room from up here." Soon Tricklane was up in the tree, too, peering into Rodney's room.

Dominion Angel Barook shivered and looked up from where he was standing over Rodney's shoulder. Rodney was seated at his desk in his room, digging through the Bible at Barook's prodding. "We're not alone tonight" said Barook, rolling his eyes from Rodney to the window in an attempt to subtly signal the kid.

Rodney very unsubtly craned his head around and peered over his shoulder into the night. "I don't see anything." Just then some leaves on the tree outside his window fluttered as two demonic beings ducked out of view.

"I see what you mean," said Tricklane, holding his crouched position in the tree underneath Rodney's window sill. "That dominion angel of his already has him reading the Bible. That's not good. But he's young. His faith can't be that well established yet. It doesn't seem like he's been through many trials. He probably doesn't fully understand the power of his righteousness in Christ. I certainly haven't heard of him before now, so it's not like he is a great prayer warrior or anything." Tricklane slowly pulled himself up to peer through the window again.

"Snack break!" announced Rodney. Barook threw his hands up in the air as Rodney pulled a Kit Kat out of his desk drawer and began munching away.

Tricklane snickered with delight. "Oh, he's a lover of snacks, is he? Good. That's one sign of being enslaved by fleshly desires. Let's hope he's slothful and lustful as well." Scumbert nodded his knobby head in agreement. Tricklane continued, "Teenage boys are frightfully easy to lead astray. Here's the plan I'll present to the boss: we discredit him with a bit of porn, some pot, and a fight at school and our work here is done. No Christians will take his advice after that. It doesn't matter how important or true his message is if his personality is full of flaws. It works every time."

"You're a—ribbit—genius!" Scumbert blurted.

"I know," sighed Tricklane happily.

♬♬

Satan, dressed in a stylish dark-grey leather flight suit, headed down a black tunnel. He was in earth's dimension, albeit underground. After a five-minute journey on his wheeled feet, he emerged into a wide, well lit, cavernous chamber deep underneath the surface of the earth. With great pride he surveyed the shiny, sleek spaceship standing upright on its rocket thrusters. It had room for only one occupant.

"I designed a beautiful ship, admiral," remarked Satan to a demonic being standing at attention nearby. "We've come a long way since the round saucer days."

"Yes, sir," answered the man-shaped fallen angel in his dark blue admiral's uniform. "Safe trip, oh angel of light." He watched Satan climb up the mobile metal staircase to the ship's entry hatch.

"Route me through Iowa this time. And send the team out to make more crop circles. We haven't done that in a while."

"Yes, sir."

Satan clambered into his space capsule and strapped himself in. He had materialized himself enough to be propelled along by the momentum of the spaceship. He had a long journey to make and didn't want to waste his own evil energy on it. This way seemed easier. Plus, it had the added benefit of perpetuating a lie he had been planting for the last hundred years or so.

Although heaven and hell were technically in the same dimension, they were very far apart. Traveling from the hellish side of things to get to the heavenly realm took a lot of time. Going through the dimension that contained earth was a good shortcut. Unfortunately, there were no more portals to heaven located on earth that Satan could access. Ever since Jesus washed the spot clean in heaven where Satan stood before God, Satan's visits there had been greatly restricted. He used to be able to attend the convocation of the angels whenever he wanted. Now he needed an appointment. And the council had reduced him to using only the Heavenlink on the dark side of the moon. "They are such jerks," he sighed to himself.

The admiral rolled the staircase out of the ship's way. He went back to his console and pressed a button which closed the hatch over Satan's head. He typed in some coordinates. The ship's launch pad tilted 30 degrees downward and to the right until the nose of the ship lined up with one of the many holes carved into the cave's rocky ceiling and walls. Another button raised a heat shield between the admiral and the ship. The heat shield was mostly for show. Fire never bothered any denizen of hell. The admiral began the countdown to launch.

"Five, four, three, two . . . we have ignition," he announced into his headset which transmitted his voice into the speakers inside Satan's helmet. The ship fired its rocket boosters and shot straight upwards into inky blackness, powering through a channel cut through the rock leading to the earth's surface. A few minutes later, the ship popped out of a dirt-covered hole in a cornfield in Iowa, taking some cornstalks with it. Cows grazing nearby looked up to see what the noise was about, and then went back to chewing their cud.

Up, up, up into space the vehicle soared, roaring through the skies and toward the dark side of the moon that never sees Earth's face. After a bumpy ride, Satan approached the huge HeavenLink located there. It was big enough to pilot his entire ship through to the heavenly dimension. As the ship spiraled through the portal, Satan could feel himself getting queasy. It wasn't so much the rolling motion as the anticipation of being in God's realm. It brought back memories. Bad ones.

"Wake up!" shouted a small demon to his partner manning the other side of this particular portal. "He's here. Snap to!" Both demons, shaped like orangutans, quickly secured the ship and helped Satan climb out of it. "Your most foulness, welcome."

"Here," muttered Satan pulling off his silver gloves and handing them to the first attendant. "I'll be back soon. I can't stand to be in this environment for very long."

"Of course, your ugliness."

As Satan rolled out of his landing dock on his wheeled feet, he saw his greeting party. A small army of cherubim—swords drawn and flaming, and wheels whirring—were there to greet the evil prince and to escort him up the street towards Gabriel's office. Adoram oversaw the procession. It was always his job to keep Satan corralled for these heavenly visits.

"How was the trip?"

"Long," said Satan, looking around at heaven and all its glory. He hadn't been here in a while. "I still don't know why you won't let me use the portals on earth."

"Because the good angels don't like being anywhere near you. I don't blame them. You're pretty horrifying. And it wasn't me. It was the council who made the final decision. You know that."

Satan turned his face toward the higher-ranking angel, and spat, "How long have you known about this boy?"

"Rodney? Only since Sunday. What are you so worried about, Lucifer? Are you afraid that Rodney, having seen the spiritual realm will be inspired to fight against you? Are you worried he will become a great spiritual warrior?"

"That pathetic child? Never," he said, keeping his cool. "No, I'm here to make a wager."

"Again?" asked Adoram, incredulous at the hubris of his old acquaintance. "Oh, you who were the seal of perfection, full of wisdom and perfect in beauty, why do this? You were in Eden, the garden of God. You were the anointed cherub. And now you come cowering before the throne of Grace to make pathetic wagers. You always lose these bets. Remember Job? And Joan of Arc? Or how about Ghandi? Or that man in Africa whose name is very hard to pronounce?"

"Yeah, it's all clicks and clacks," Satan laughed.

"That's him! Anyway, the list goes on and on. I can't even count how many times you've lost."

"I'll win eventually," said Satan, nonplussed.

"No, you won't!" said Adoram, vehemently. Then, more calmly: "This all ends with you being thrown into a lake of fire. You've read the Bible. You know that."

"I know no such thing. The Bible is full of lies. And anyway, I can't just give up now, can I?" asked Satan smoothly. "What would be the fun in that? Skip that whole epic battle? Poppycock!" Satan waved his hand dismissively at the thought.

By now the two creatures had made their way up to the door of Gabriel's cottage. "He's expecting you," said Adoram. "God told him you were coming."

"You know that whole omniscient, omnipresent thing really isn't sporting."

"Hey, nobody said you had to get all proud-hearted and power-hungry because of your beauty and start a revolution. You corrupted your wisdom for the sake of your splendor. I told you back then that it was going to get you kicked out."

"You always were a buzzkill," Satan said over his shoulder as he strode arrogantly into the entryway of Gabriel's palace.

Adoram noticed a choir of angels standing along the staircase ready to sing. Gabriel was in the doorway of his office, towering over the prince of the earth. "Long time no see, Belial," he commented as Satan entered his office.

"Those choir angels better keep their yaps shut while I'm here," he snorted while settling himself onto the high couch. "Is this Earl Grey tea? You know I hate tisanes."

"Nothing herbal for you, I remember," said Gabriel sitting down next to him and motioning for Adoram to take a chair next to them.

"Here's the deal," Satan blurted out. "If I can turn Rodney against God, I get another thousand years to rule earth before He returns."

"What no 'Hello, Gabriel. How've you been Gabriel? Sorry about that whole rebellion I led'? Oh Beelzebub, you never change. Why do you think the free will that God gave to people will always work in your favor?"

"Because most of the time, people choose not to believe in Him—or me, for that matter, which makes my job easy."

"Yes, but when they do choose to believe, their love for God is deeper and truer than any forced honor ever could be. But you wouldn't know anything about that. You rule through fear and deception. No one truly loves you."

"Oh, I hate coming here," sighed Satan, rolling his eyes. "So, let's just make this deal and let me get out of here before any praise songs start up." Satan eyed the choir nervously.

"They're just here to make sure you leave on time," said Gabriel. "What does our side get if Rodney resists you completely?"

"Another very strong saint who has been tested in the fire who will be loyal to God unto the end."

Gabriel paused dramatically and then finally announced, "I have been authorized to tell you that you have seven days."

"Starting tomorrow," added Satan.

"Right. You may only tempt Rodney once per day. Each temptation session must be an hour or less."

"Fine," sighed Satan taking a sip of tea from his cup.

"Then we have a deal," announced Gabriel. Time for you to go now."

Adoram, from his wingback chair, smiled toward the choir and said, "I feel a Beethoven hymn coming on."

Satan clapped his hands over his ears and yelled, "Ahhhhhhh, I can't hear you," as he wheeled out of the room, out the door of the palace, and out of the front garden of the cottage. He kept his hands over his ears all the way back down the street toward his landing dock, chased by an army of cherubim.

To Adoram, Gabriel said, "You should probably get down there and watch Rodney's back. The Evil One won't win, but he's good at what he does. Seven days of temptation and condemnation from him is hard to resist. Help Rodney stay focused on Jesus and His redeeming blood. Remind the boy of the power of the righteousness imputed to him through Jesus' death. Teach him that all of his sins are forgiven—past and present and future—so that he can walk in faith. And make sure he doesn't fall off a cliff or anything."

♫♫

The song "Greatness of Our God" by the Newsboys played over Rodney's iPod speakers in his room. It was dark outside. Rodney's parents had gone to bed. He was still up, after a long day that involved a frog-shaped devil and a guardian angel who was trying to cram six years of Sunday school lessons into one evening. Rodney was sitting at his desk reading from his Bible while Barook, the dominion angel assigned by God to keep Rodney alive and well, looked on.

"It says, 'Put on the whole armor of God that you may be able to stand against the wiles of the devil'." He looked up. "Do you really think some demons might come here and attack me?"

"I think it's a distinct possibility. Adoram sent a message to me from heaven."

"How did he do that?"

"We angels can share our thoughts with each other when we need to."

"Wait. Whoa. Hold on. You can communicate telepathically? Are you kidding me?"

"I jest not, my mortal friend, coiled in weakness and flesh. I wouldn't call it 'telepathically' but we can send messages to each other across time and space. We communicate with God the same way. We can also traverse time and space very quickly when we need to. It takes a lot of energy, so mostly we use portals to get to heaven and back."

"What? There's a portal to heaven that you use? Where is it?"

"I am not at liberty to disclose such sensitive information to humans."

"Oh, c'mon. You can tell me. I won't give your secret away."

"You won't give the secret away because you won't have the secret."

"Huh!" Rodney huffed in frustration. "Fine. What did Adoram say when he sent his message to you?"

"Satan has shown his bare bodkin."

"Wait! Satan mooned you? Why would he do that?"

"Um, maybe those words are too archaic. I must try harder to right my language. What I mean is, Satan has shown his plan, as plainly as unsheathing his dagger. He is resolved to tempt you mightily, he and his minions."

"Oh, that's great! Just great. Just what I need right now."

"I agree. I devoutly wish we had more time. Your training is nowhere near its completion. You still believe your actions have something to do with your righteousness. You haven't yet learned to rest in your faith and trust God. I dread their coming."

"You dread their coming? What about me? I'm freaking out over here!" Rodney got up from his desk and paced back and forth across his room, nearly tripping over the backpack he had dropped in a random spot on the floor Friday afternoon.

"You do look pale—paler than usual. Let us turn back to the truth and comfort of God's word. Satan is lies. He and his workers shall lead you, if you let them, to wrong thoughts. You must know you are an heir because Jesus rose up and conquered sin and death. You must know, as you face a sea of troubles, what your idol Clint Eastwood spoke of in the movie *Unforgiven*." Here Barook added a thick Texan accent to his voice, "It ain't about derservin'."

Rodney burst into laughter. "Oh snap! My angel is doing Clint Eastwood!" He pounded the desk with his fist.

Barook continued unfazed, "Remember that you have God's favor, unmerited by you, unearned by you. Know that we are here, taking up arms for you. Know what you saw, that prayer works."

"So, if I ask God for your help, you can protect me, right?"

"What does your Bible say about that?"

Rodney read aloud, "'Stand, therefore, having girded your waist with truth, having put on the breastplate of righteousness, and having shod your feet with the preparation of the gospel of peace.' So that's why you have me reading the Bible." He continued, "'above all taking the shield of faith with which you will be able to quench all the fiery darts of the wicked one.' Oh my gosh! I saw those fiery darts. 'Put on salvation as your helmet, and take the sword of the spirit which is the word of God.' I hope that sword cuts deep, because I'm going to need all the help I can get. Maybe I should fast. Didn't I read somewhere about a demon being cast out by prayer and fasting? It's gonna be tough, but I think I can do it."

"As I've told you, it's not your strength, or sweat, or arms that will win this. It's not your work which frees you from sin's grasp."

"Oh, right. I already forgot. It's God's strength, and I need to learn to draw on that. But I feel like I should do something. Maybe fasting will help. I mean, it's better than running a needle through the eye of a camel. I'm pretty sure I read that somewhere. It sounds awful."

Barook just stared at his pupil and shook his head. "Stand in God's grace, forgiven. Call on His strength, not yours."

"I'll start fasting tomorrow morning," said Rodney, ignoring Barook. "This isn't going to be easy. Tomorrow is waffle day." Rodney switched off his iPod and threw himself onto his bed. "Hey Bazooka, can you hit the light?"

♪♪♪♪

The Starbucks at the corner of Ventura Boulevard and Allott Avenue was teeming with people. The line snaked from the counter out the front door. The tables on the patio were filling up fast. Screenwriters, in-between-jobs at the moment, had their laptops open and were clicking away. Inside, three actors discussed an upcoming play they were to perform. Two demons sat chuckling at a communal table nearby.

"And that half-caff soy latte is now a fully caffeinated dairy drink," said the lord of the darkness eyeing one of the baristas behind the counter.

"You know, your grace, I've always wondered why you enjoy these little frustrations so much," said Tricklane, Satan's right-hand angel.

"Unhappy people sin more, Tricklane. It's as simple as that. No matter how good someone's financial situation or lifestyle or job, these little frustrations can add up and ruin their days, their weeks, their lives. What seems to you inconsequential, is just one more link in a chain of bondage called dissatisfaction. I'm destroying attitudes—creating a feeling of not having enough. See that man in the suit over there? I want to show him how much there is to be ungrateful for before he climbs back into his BMW to continue his morning commute in an infuriating tangle of traffic."

"But he has to pass that homeless man before he reaches his $80,000 car. Won't that give him some perspective? Wouldn't it be better just to wreck his car and disable him?"

"Really, Tricklane? Have I taught you nothing? First of all, there are zero angels in here at the moment. None of these people are Christians. I'm sure some will come in later, but as for this batch of humans, no one is teaching them the concept of gratefulness. And even if they did hear it somewhere, who are the godless going to be grateful to? The universe? You and I both know it doesn't count if they're not actually grateful to God, which is why we work so hard to remove his name from everything."

"Of course, your grossness. I know that."

"Secondly, everything is relative. Most people have a hard time keeping perspective. They generally don't compare themselves to the homeless or the jobless or the desperately poor. People tend to compare themselves to their peers and those above them in station. Spill some coffee on that woman's silk skirt—like so—and it will threaten her status at work." Just at that moment, a blonde woman in a blue silk skirt was bumped by the BMW-owning man in the suit. Some of her coffee splattered onto her skirt; brown streaks slowly expanded into a sea of blue.

"Oh no!" she cried.

"Now she has to decide whether it's worse to show up with a ruined skirt or to be late because she went home and changed," continued Satan.

"But that isn't sinful, my disgusting lord."

"Not yet. But tell me, Tricklane, who are the bullies of the world?"

The blonde stormed out past the apologetic suited man who was left holding napkins up in the air.

"Well, people who live in the gutter don't usually bully," Tricklane said, more to himself than to Satan. Then, after a few seconds of working out the definition in his head, he came out with, "Bullies are popular men and women in positions of power who want to consolidate and confirm that power. Sometimes they're in high school and sometimes they're in the board room."

"Exactly. But these powerful, popular people—like her and like him," Satan pointed to the blonde woman and the man in the suit "have to be unhappy to bully. They have to feel frustrated. Grateful people, even powerful ones, don't torture others. You see?"

"Yes sir, I do. But you have so many powers and principalities who do this work for you. Why bother?"

"Like any good CEO, I like to keep my hand in the business at all levels." Satan leaned back in his chair, invisible to all around him, and smiled.

"Of course, sir. I understand. What about Rodney? He's not powerful. Do you like my plan for attacking him?"

"I don't need it. I'll use the tool I employ on every Christian: the law. I'll show him how he doesn't measure up. He'll feel guilty. He'll obsess over not sinning. He'll sin even more because of it. Rodney is an insecure, untested, unready-for-life teenager who has no grasp on the truth of his own holiness. This is literally going to be a piece of cake."

Chapter 6

*The people who know their God shall be strong
and carry out great exploits.*

~ Daniel 11:32

Rodney's stomach was growling. He had endured the agony of passing up his dad's homemade waffles this morning, but the day was wearing on without relief. The orange juice he allowed himself wasn't cutting it. He had somehow lived through wood shop and biology. But the students sitting next to him in physics class at Birmingham Community Charter High School were starting to notice the protestations emanating from his midsection. This was unbearable. It was only 10:20 a.m.

The pretty girl sitting next to him laughed when Rodney's stomach produced another gurgling roar. "Child, you're hungry!" Sharise chided. Rodney looked up and weakly smiled at her. She had short, smooth, dark hair and Rodney liked the shape of her coffee-ice-cream-hued face. There was a guardian angel, who looked like a sweet old black woman, sitting on top of Sharise's desk. Rodney thought about how there's nothing more comforting in the entire world than a sweet, old black lady. He was glad to see her sitting there.

It was at that moment that Rodney realized he had never paid attention to Sharise's faith before. He had known her for two years but he hadn't noticed she was a Christian. He just thought she was nice. He made a mental note to pay more attention to people's belief systems in the future. And then he realized he didn't have to work at it. It was all completely obvious to him now. If someone had an angel hanging around, he or she was a believer.

He wondered if the demons were proof of anything. Like the buzzard-shaped one perched on Mr. Thaxton's shoulder right now. Rodney wanted to ask Barook about it, but he didn't want the teacher to hear him whispering and assign him pushups, so he let it go. Just then, the short stubby teacher was launching into a lecture on the universe.

"Okay dummies, who thinks outer space is expanding?" Most of the hands went up. "Good! You five who didn't raise your hands, drop and give me ten pushups." The kids were used to this kind of mind-body drill so they complied without a peep while Mr. Thaxton continued his line of questioning.

"And who thinks the universe is expanding ever more slowly since the Big Bang due to the constricting forces of gravity?" Six kids raised their hands cautiously while looking around the room, hoping more hands would shoot up. Rodney had managed to complete his required reading last week so he kept his hand down.

"No!" shouted Mr. Thaxton. "Don't you remember 1998 and the Hubble showing us that the rate of expansion is accelerating? Drop and give me ten." Now eleven kids were on the floor, almost kissing the linoleum, their arms straining to complete the physical task assigned them.

"So what force is strong enough to overcome gravity and keep the universe expanding at not just a constant rate, but at an ever-increasing rate?" he queried the 20 or so kids left sitting in their chairs.

"Dark energy?" offered Sharise with a bit of uncertainty in her voice.

"Good girl. And what's the difference between dark matter and dark energy?" He pointed to a freckle-faced, heavy-set boy near the back of the class. "Mike?"

"A Red Bull, sir?" As the class cracked up and Mr. Thaxton opened his mouth to yell for more pushups, Mike rapidly added, "No, just kidding. Dark energy makes up about 70% of the universe and dark matter makes up about 25%. Dark energy is pulling the universe apart while dark matter has enough mass to exert gravitational pull. It's matter, not energy, but scientists aren't sure what it's made up of. It might be something like WIMPS—weakly interacting massive particles."

"Good enough, boy." Thaxton nodded his approval. The rest of the class had finished their pushups and climbed back into their chairs by now. "Who wants to tell me about WIMPS and MACHOs?"

As a beautiful Latina named Selefina struggled to answer the question, Rodney's mind wandered back to angels and demons. He could see a demonic snake coiled around Selefina's neck. Demons certainly felt like dark energy to him. He hoped they didn't make up 70% of the universe. He had noticed that demons could be hanging out on both Christians and non-Christians. It was disconcerting for him. He longed for some light energy and began praying in his head. "Thank you, God, for sending Bazooka to look after me for all these years. He cares so much about me and never leaves my side. It weirds me out when I take a shower, but I get it. And he's learned to stand on the other side of the shower curtain now. So, thank You, Lord, for Your protection through him and through Adoram and through all the rest of the angelic host. Thank you for creating angels in the first place. You must have known we would need them. Amen."

∫∫∫∫

Rodney's stomach had given up on sending auditory signals by the time classes let out for the afternoon. Instead it just hung there listlessly while the rest of Rodney changed his clothes after gym class. He ambled hungrily out to the school's parking lot, his backpack filled with books bumping along on his shoulder. His course took him through the outer edge of the baseball field. It was already in use by the school's boy's baseball team. Coach Tyson was yelling, "What are you buffoons doing out there? Throw the ball at a person, not the space between people!"

Barook, walking next to Rodney, had his eye on the practice session. He knew a potential threat when he saw one. Sure enough, a stray ball thrown by a muscular, dark-haired teen came whizzing toward Rodney's head. Rodney, as usual, was completely oblivious to the danger he was in. Barook quickly put his foot out, materializing it just long enough to trip Rodney and make him fall on his face in the soft grass. The baseball flew safely by, now five feet over his grounded head.

"Dang it!" yelled Rodney, picking himself and his backpack up off the ground. "I thought you were supposed to keep me from harm, Bazooka! What the heck happened?"

"I'm sorry," Barook replied, without explaining further. He didn't need Rodney to always know the whole story. He just needed Rodney to be as safe as possible. In the background the coach yelled, "What did I just say, Dawkins?"

At that moment, Barook and Rodney were joined by Kim, Rodney's best friend.

"Hey avocado toast."

"Hey French toast," Rodney responded, continuing their usual greeting game as they made their way together toward the parking lot.

"No, that's a breakfast food. The category is clearly trendy appetizers or avocado-based smacks. Try again."

"Oh, sorry. Hey avocado."

"No. This fasting thing is really distracting you."

"K, I got it. Hey guacamole."

"That's better."

Barook dropped back to walk behind the boys, joining Koram, Kim's guardian angel. They chatted softly about the day and Rodney's attempt at fasting.

"Wait!" Rodney came to a dead halt, sticking his arm out in front of Kim's chest to stop his forward momentum as well. "There's a guy standing next to my car."

Kim squinted toward the custardy orange 1975 Pacer Sundowner at the back of the parking lot. "Where? I don't see anyone."

"There, the guy in the really nice suit. He looks exactly like Jude Law."

"The actor? The one who played Watson in *Sherlock Holmes* with Robert Downey Jr.?"

"Yeah. He was also Dumbledore in *Fantastic Beasts*, and Yon-Rogg in *Captain Marvel*, remember?"

"Yeah! No, I don't see him."

"Oh, great. That means he's probably a spirit being. I wonder what this is all about. Let me do all the talking, K?"

"Dude, I can't see these supernatural beings or hear them, so I think that's a given."

Rodney cautiously approached his car at the edge of the school's parking lot. Barook offered instructions on the way.

"Demons are angels of light. They use beauty, charm, and wit to fool you. Be careful."

"Jude Law is a demon?" asked Rodney incredulously.

Barook didn't want to reveal that the being who looked like Jude Law was actually Satan himself. "No, this demon seems like Jude Law to you because you regard that actor as handsome, charming, and stylish."

"I do?" asked Rodney.

"You must" the angel responded.

"Well, maybe I do think he's pretty chill."

"Keep your tent flaps closed. Wait. Let me update that. Keep your yap shut. Close your pie hole. Demons cannot read your mind. Nor can angels for that matter. We are privy only to what you speak aloud." By the time Barook finished his speech, the group had come face to face with the lord of the darkness.

"Cheerio. Cupcake?" asked Jude Law. A box from Sprinkles bakery sat on the roof of Rodney's car. Kim saw the lid of the box blow open with a gust of wind but heard none of what Satan said.

"Banana, chocolate-marshmallow, or mocha flavor?" asked Satan.

Rodney's stomach cried aloud with desire. "I, uh . . ."

"Here, try the chocolate-marshmallow. It has dark chocolate cake, marshmallow cream, and bittersweet chocolate ganache on top." Kim watched a cupcake float out of the box and hover inches from Rodney's face. He was dying to ask what was going on, but before he could ask, Rodney's hands—working in cahoots with his empty, angry stomach—had grabbed the treat, ripped off the paper liner, and shoved half of it into his mouth. "Oh mab, that's goob," the curly-haired, freckle-faced boy mumbled while chewing and swallowing. He attacked the rest of the cupcake as if the act of devouring it would solve more than just his hunger. Kim laughed. Barook rolled his eyes. And Koram shook his angel head.

"Yes, they're delicious," smiled the demon who resembled—and sounded like—an attractive middle-aged actor from South London. "Try the red velvet."

Exactly one minute later Rodney had eaten six cupcakes. Jude Law held up a bottle of cold milk with a sly smile. "Thirsty?"

"Fine!" Rodney shouted. He grabbed the plastic bottle of milk that seemed to Kim to be magically floating in mid-air. While cracking open the security-sealed screw-top, Rodney groused, "My day of fasting has been a total fail, anyway. Might as well go for it." This was killing Kim, but he kept quiet and wondered what would happen next.

"Yes, exactly, my friend," the accuser purred in his perfect British accent. "God is already disappointed in you. Why bother trying so hard?"

Rodney wiped his mouth with his hand and looked over at Barook. The angel reminded him, "There is no condemnation in Christ, Rodney. Be not afraid. You have been forgiven your failures. You are not under the law, but the new covenant of grace!" Rodney looked down at his feet in shame and nodded, not quite convinced of this truth.

"Lord, I thank you that where sin exists, grace abounds" prayed Barook.

"Shall we go for a ride?" asked the charming man in the Prada suit.

Rodney shot Barook a questioning look. Barook just shrugged his shoulders and let Rodney make the decision. Barook had been informed by Adoram of the wager Satan made with God, so he wasn't going to interfere.

"Sure," said Rodney, wondering where this day was going. He looked over at a confused but patient Kim. "You can take a ride with me. We're going to drop my friend off at home. Then we can hang out." Rodney unlocked and opened the passenger door of his car. Kim moved to get inside, but Jude Law smoothly slid into the front seat first. Rodney grabbed Kim's shoulder. He didn't want Kim too close to Satan. Plus, it would be so weird for him to see a spirit on top of his best friend. He wasn't in the mood to deal with that. "Why don't you ride in the back seat today? Jude Law has shotgun." Rodney swiped the box of cupcakes off the roof of his car and walked around to the driver's side. Kim followed.

"Did you just say that Jude Law has shotgun?" asked Kim as he climbed into the too-small car.

"Yeah. You want a cupcake? I have to warn you, though. They kinda taste like shame."

"Sure." Kim grabbed the box, selected a treat, and started eating it. "These shame cakes are good! How did Jude Law get them here? Isn't he a spirit?"

Satan answered. "Yes, I'm a spirit, but I can manifest as a human if and when I need to. I can also manifest as a voice on the phone, which takes less energy. Food delivery services aren't hard to come by in Los Angeles. Getting them to deliver to an empty car in a parking lot was a bit tricky, but I worked it out. I told them I was surprising my friend."

Rodney knew that Kim couldn't hear any of this, so he translated the speech this way: "GrubHub."

"Oh, smart!" said Kim.

Barook and Koram began hovering over the Pacer when Rodney asked them to stuff their large frames into the back seat next to Kim. "I might need to ask you guys some questions and I can't see you through the roof. Do you mind?"

Barook and Koram looked at each other, nodded, and manifested themselves just enough to be carried along by the car. Then they climbed in.

Rodney exited the school's parking lot and took a left on Balboa Boulevard, a busy street teeming with cars and small strip malls. Students were walking and riding their scooters and skateboards up and down the sidewalks. After several blocks, Rodney eased his Pacer onto Sherman Way, a main artery running across the Valley floor. It was dotted with huge pine trees, towering oaks, and other large non-native species of trees that thrived when watered. The trees helped the street look less industrial than it was, but not quite all the way to charming. The car passed The Church on the Way and Rodney took a left onto a small side street. A few turns later he ended up on Cantlay Street in front of a 1950's-era single-story home with a birdhouse built into the peak of the roof above the garage. It was a style of house pioneered by the developer William Mellenthin. "Here you go, dude." Rodney got out of the car and flipped his seat forward so Kim could get out of the two-door bubble.

"Thanks, man. I have some websites to build today or I'd stay with you. Do you want me to blow it off?"

"No. You need to do your work. You're still paying off that new laptop you bought, remember? And anyway, this would just be frustrating for you, not knowing what's going on the whole time."

"I guess." Kim got out of the car and stood on his curb. "Are you sure you don't need me, though?"

"Bazooka's got my back."

"Who?"

"My guardian angel. That's his name. Well, that's what I call him, anyway."

"Oh, right. Well, good. Text me when you get a chance. I need to hear all about this."

"Yep." Rodney climbed back into his ridiculous orange car and waved goodbye to Kim and his ever-present helper, Koram.

Then he fished in the back seat for another cupcake. "Where to peeps?"

∬∬

Rodney had a feeling he wouldn't be getting any homework done today. He had just met Satan, who appeared to be the handsome English actor Jude Law. The evil angel of light had already tricked Rodney into breaking his fast and it was only 3:45 p.m. Rodney felt like a loser, a failure, and an unsophisticated idiot. Luckily for him, he didn't even know it was the prince of this world who was paying him a visit. He thought it was just some random demon— and that was enough to give him anxiety.

Rodney's sunset-hued Pacer was heading west on Sherman Way in the San Fernando Valley of Los Angeles in an area of town called Van Nuys. In the front seat next to Rodney sat the devil, the cherub who fell from heaven like lightning. In the back seat was Barook, Rodney's nervous dominion angel. Satan was suggesting that they all head back to Rodney's place to relax and smoke a little something, when Adoram—a six-winged seraph angel—came flying through the windshield of Rodney's bubble-shaped car. Barook breathed an audible sigh of relief at the sight of his powerful supervising angel. Adoram hovered in front of Satan's face and said, "How about you move to the back seat?"

Satan complied, knowing that Adoram outranked him in the angelic order, and also was more powerful than he. Now was not the time to put up a fight. Satan grumbled, "You again? Can't get enough of me, old friend?"

"Not when you're messing with a saint in my territory."

"Adoram! It's good to see you," exclaimed Rodney.

"It's good to see you also, Rodney."

Rodney whispered, "This demon seems nice, but he did get me to break my fast already. I guess I'm being a spiritual wimp instead of a spiritual warrior."

Jude Law smiled from the back seat. Adoram's face hardened with resolve. "God knows what He's doing. He won't allow you to be tempted beyond your strength. I'm here to help you. Barook is here to help you. God will give you power. What more do you need?"

"Are you kidding me? What more do I need?" Rodney practically shouted. "An army of angels. Um, more self-control. Some extra smarts wouldn't hurt. A better-looking face. Less acne. Nicer clothes. Some coordination and skill at sports."

"Some confidence," Barook chimed in from the back seat.

Jude Law smiled again.

"This demon wants you to feel impotent," Adoram continued.

"Ahhhh!" Rodney screamed while gripping the steering wheel tightly. "I'm impotent? Are you kidding me? This is a disaster!"

"No, no, no," said Adoram as Jude Law chuckled, and Barook shook his head and lowered his eyes to the floor. "You are not powerless because God will deliver you from the perilous pestilence. He shall cover you with His feathers, and under His wings you shall take refuge. No evil shall befall you. He has given His angels charge over you. You shall trample the serpent under your foot."

"Yes, you have nothing to fear from me, Rodney" Jude Law purred from the back seat. "You need to relax. Have you heard of the medicinal qualities of cannabis? It's an herb that can calm you down and help you deal with these anxieties and troublesome emotions. It's all natural, and in California it's perfectly legal."

"You mean pot?" asked Rodney.

"Don't you think it would help you right now?" asked the serpent of old.

"Maybe, I don't know. I've never smoked it before."

Adoram could see where this was going. He couldn't tell Satan to leave or to shut up because God Himself allowed Satan to be here to tempt Rodney, but he could try to foil these evil plans and turn them into lessons. "Why don't we stop at that pot clinic on the corner of Sepulveda and Sherman Way? It's got a hookah bar on the back patio. That way Rodney can sample a few different varieties."

"You're chill with this?" Rodney asked Adoram.

"If it helps you calm down, yes."

"Wonderful idea," said Satan. Barook kept quiet while wondering how Adoram would turn this situation to Rodney's good. He wasn't sure it would work.

∫∫∫∫

Rodney pulled into a run-down strip mall. It wasn't far from Rodney's school and some of his classmates visited this place on a regular basis. The tiny parking lot was jammed with cars. One of the storefront windows displayed a bright green plus sign—the sure indicator of a place that sold marijuana. Rodney eased his ancient Pacer into a too-small parking space and squeezed out of his half-open door, trying not to bang it against the car next to him. His troupe of supernatural companions simply floated out through the car's windows.

Rodney pulled open the door of Healthy Life Collective. In front of him was a counter displaying mason jars full of marijuana buds of all varieties. Glass pipes were on a lower shelf. A hallway on the right led to a back patio. Rodney told the clerk behind the counter that he was going to the hookah bar in back. He couldn't help but notice the demon octopus hanging onto the clerk's head and the demon sloth on his back. There was also a demon goat jumping around his feet.

The patio that housed the hookah bar was fenced in for privacy but roofless so the copious amounts of smoke generated in its space could waft up and out. The overriding aroma was one of skunk spray. Small pockets of bubblegum and mint hit Rodney's nose, but mostly all he could smell was skunky smoke. He chose a small empty table and sat down. A cute waitress approached him. Supernatural frogs jumped all over her shoulders and hopped around her feet. "What can I get for you?"

"I'll take the daily special, the Blueberry Yum Yum," said Rodney pointing to the chalkboard on the wall, trying to look cool although he had no idea what he had just ordered. He had never smoked a cigarette, much less a joint or a water pipe before. He had no clue what different flavors of weed smelled or tasted like. He figured anything with such a silly name couldn't be all that bad. Silently his angel companions stood around his table. Satan slipped into the seat across from him. "If you need help, just let me know," he offered. Looking around he added, "It's glamorously dirty in here." Rodney was thankful no one else could see or hear this crazy demon.

He let his eyes drift over the people sitting around him. Large bongs with multiple tubes sat bubbling on tabletops. At one table of middle-aged businessmen he saw swarms of demon locusts flying into the hookahs and being sucked into the men through the stems of the pipes. His eyes whipped over to another table of teenage guys sharing two hookahs. Through one hookah, frog-shaped evil spirits flew into a brown-haired boy. Adoram clocked Rodney's stare. He leaned in and whispered in Rodney's ear, "That young man doesn't even know he has bipolar disorder.

These mind-altering drugs will make his condition worse. He's in for a scary ride over the next week. So are his friends and his family."

"How are the demons getting inside people?" Rodney quietly asked the angel.

"Demons need permission to inhabit a person, just like the Holy Spirit does. Drugs, alcohol, mind-bending mushrooms—they all weaken a person's defenses. All a demon has to do is ask, and poof—it's in. Sadly, the wicked shall do wickedly and none of them shall understand their wickedness. But the wise shall understand. Pray for them that they may come to their senses and escape the snare of the devil, having been taken captive by him to do his will."

"Oh, that won't happen to you, Rodney," said Satan, butting into the conversation. "You're stronger than these fools. You're as smart as an Audrey Hepburn dress." Just then the waitress set down Rodney's Blueberry Yum Yum-loaded hookah in front of him with a smile. "Give it a try," Satan prodded. "See, there aren't any demons in yours."

"Not right now there aren't," said Rodney, "but after a few tokes I won't care if there are demons in that hookah or not. Forget it. I'm open minded, but not to the point that I want my brain leaking out. That ain't it," he said to his invisible companions, dropping some cash on the table. "I'm done here. I've seen enough."

"Thanks a lot, Buzzkill," Jude Law said to the seraph angel as they followed Rodney out the door. Barook let out a sigh of relief.

Rodney squeezed back into his orange car. He noticed that demon flies were buzzing all around him. "Adoram, how do I get rid of these?"

"Wash your feet in the water of the word."

"Good idea." Rodney turned his key in the ignition and switched on the radio. The old-fashioned dial was tuned to 95.9 FM The Fish, a Christian radio station. A song by the David Crowder Band, "O Praise Him," blared through the ancient, staticky car speakers. Rodney sang along in his cracked, teenage voice. He did not have perfect pitch, but he did have enthusiasm.

"O praise Him,

O praise Him,

He is holy,

He is holy!"

Satan grimaced in pain as the angels chimed in on the hallelujahs. "I—I, I need to be somewhere more important," he shouted, flying with great speed out of the little tangerine-colored car. The demon flies swarmed out directly afterward.

"That was cray cray," said Rodney, turning down the radio. "I'm glad he's gone, though, and I can put this whole temptation thing behind me." Adoram and Barook shared a look. Neither one of them wanted to tell Rodney that he had six more days of this in front of him. They weren't entirely sure he would make it through.

♫♫

It was almost 6 p.m. on Tuesday, a warm April day in Los Angeles. Rodney was knocking on the door of his best friend's house. Kim's little sister answered it.

"Hey Soo, oh, I mean Sue," Rodney said to the sixteen-year-old girl.

"You know they sound the same, right?" she retorted. "You are so cringy."

Kim's whole name was Soo-Hee Kim, and his sister was named Soo-Ah Kim. Kim's first-grade teacher never really grasped the concept that Korean surnames are listed first. So, she tagged Soo-Hee with "Kim." It stuck. When Kim got older, he didn't want to be confused with his sister, Soo-Ah, so he let everyone keep calling him by his last name.

His sister wasn't so accommodating. She wanted an American name, so she pestered her parents into changing her first name to Sue, which of course sounds exactly like Soo, but is for some reason, easier for Americans to pronounce. Rodney had known her since she was two, so it was hard for him to make the switch in his head, even though he never really had to.

Knowing Rodney wasn't here to visit her, Sue said, "He's in his room," while pointing down the hall and walking away.

"Thanks," said Rodney, following the hallway to its end. He burst into his friend's room and closed the door behind him.

Barook floated through the closed door and settled into a quiet conversation with Koram, Kim's guardian angel.

"You are not gonna believe what I just saw," Rodney said, flopping backwards onto Kim's bed. Kim was sitting at his desk.

"Do tell," said Kim, closing his laptop and turning his full attention to his freaked-out friend.

"Drugs are bad, dude," said Rodney staring at the ceiling.

"Yeah. We knew that already, dude."

"No, I mean really, really bad."

"What happened? Give me the deets. Did the demon inject you with heroin or something?"

"What? No! No, it wasn't that bad. He tried to get me to smoke pot. But when I went to the collective, I saw all these demons getting into people through their hookahs. It was cray cray. I had no idea that drugs were a gateway for demon possession. It was awful. I got out of there as fast as I could."

"Well, I didn't know that either, but now that you say it, it kinda makes sense. I mean, the whole point of pot and alcohol and meth and stuff is to check out mentally, obvi. So, I guess when you do that, you leave yourself vulnerable. That's really scary."

"It scared me straight, man."

"You were already straight. You've never done drugs in your life."

"Yeah, but still."

"Calm down, buddy. You're safe now. Is he gone? The Jude Law guy?"

"Yeah, he's gone. He took off when I started singing praise songs."

"Well, that's a neat trick. You should keep that in your back pocket for when things get too intense. Do you think he's coming back?"

"I have no idea. I hope not. I mean, he's chill, but he also makes me so nervous."

"You've only spent like, an hour, with him. How bad can it be?"

"You have no idea."

"I guess I don't. But you have your angel with you, right?"

"Bazooka? Yeah, he's here. He's talking to your angel."

"Well, isn't he helping you out? Can't he answer some of your questions? I mean, if I were you, I'd be asking him all kinds of questions. Like, what is heaven like? Has he seen the face of God? Does he know the future? Does he understand why we all are so fragile and pathetic? Why don't we see miracles much more oft—"

"Stop!" screamed Rodney. "I can't even! It's all too much!"

"Whoah. Just try to relax. No more questions, I promise. What do you need? What do you want to do?"

"Can we just play Call of Duty for an hour?"

"Sure. And I'll ask my mom if you can stay for dinner."

"What are you having?"

"Bulgogi."

"I'm starting to feel better already," said Rodney, his face relaxing into a smile at the thought of Kim's mom's sweet, marinated, grilled beef over sticky white rice.

Chapter 7

For His eyes are on the ways of man,
and He sees all his steps.

~ Job 34:21

Rodney's round, bright orange Pacer wove its way through thick Wednesday morning traffic. He and his best friend Kim were on their way to Birmingham Community Charter High School. Two guardian angels sat in the back of the old car. Their large, seven-foot frames pushed their knees up to their chests in the cramped space. Rodney preferred them to ride inside the car versus flying over it, as was their wont. He liked to keep an eye on them. He wasn't sure what they would do, but he wanted to be able to see them, even though they were constantly distracting him. They sat quietly listening to the boys' conversation.

"You still haven't told your parents about your new superpower?" asked Kim, surprised.

"I wouldn't call it super. Maybe super stinky. It makes me feel crazy. I have to work so hard to keep it together when other people are around. I'm worried someone's going to have me committed."

"Yeah, there's that," said Kim.

"And then, because of this super stinky power—that I didn't ask for—I get demons visiting me. And all they want to do is trip me up and get me sent to hell for eternity."

"I don't think even Satan himself can get you sent to hell. I'm pretty sure you can't lose your salvation."

"Yes, and again, yes," said Barook loudly from the back seat.

Rodney looked back at Barook and Koram next to him, nodding his angel head. Turning to Kim, he said, "The angels are on your side, as usual. I don't know why this didn't happen to you."

"Maybe because I'd spend all day asking them about heaven, and God, and my purpose here on earth."

"Yeah, you're boring like that."

"Well, what are you gonna do?"

"I don't know. I quit fasting. I guess I'll just have to pray a lot. Barook wants me to read the Bible more, but I have a lot of schoolwork to do." With that Rodney threw a look at his back seat.

"I hear you," said Kim. "On the other hand, Jude Law might come back."

"He's not really that scary, though, now that I think about it. He looks so chill, you know? And he hasn't done me any harm. He seems nice enough."

Rodney maneuvered his Pacer into a parking space in the school parking lot and the boys made their way to the open hallways where their lockers were. As they picked out the books and papers they would need for their first classes, Rodney noticed Mr. Thaxton, his physics teacher, walking by muttering, "I hate my life."

"Hey," Rodney nudged Kim. "See Mr. Thaxton? He's got a demon buzzard on his shoulder. Bazooka told me yesterday it's a spirit of depression."

"Well that explains a lot," said Kim.

"And you know Sharise?"

"Yeah?"

"She's got a sweet old lady guardian angel, so that means she's a Christian."

"Well, obvi."

"You knew that?"

"You didn't?"

"Uh no. I gotta get to wood shop. See you later."

"Later, man."

Barook followed Rodney through the throng of high school students toward his first class. In the open hallway that had pillars holding up a roof over a cement floor, Rodney encountered Selefina, the devastatingly pretty Latina from his physics class.

She still had that demon snake writhing around her neck and down one arm. Rodney wondered what that signified when she asked him, "Do you have any lunch money? I forgot mine this morning."

Rodney dug in his pocket and fished out the $5 his mom had left him for the cafeteria lunch today. He handed it over with little hesitation. Selefina was so pretty and Rodney was so easily dazzled. As she grabbed the bill out of his hand, her demon snake hissed and struck at his fingers. Barook's wing was there instantly to protect Rodney from further harm, but the snake had stung him slightly. "Ow!" Rodney yelled as he reflexively jumped back.

"What?" Selefina asked noncommittally. "Did my nails scratch you?"

"Uh, I guess so," answered Rodney, trying to cover his blunder. "No prob."

Selefina walked away without apologizing or thanking him for the money. Rodney was smiling as he watched her go. Barook, forgetting himself for a moment, slipped back into his old vernacular and said, "'Tis a selfish spirit which knows not love. Its bites can sting and eat a dove like you, lad."

Rodney shrugged and turned into a large room equipped with table saws, sawhorses, lathes, planers, and all manner of equipment to cut and shape wood. He pulled his project out of its storage locker. It was supposed to be a side table, but it was still woefully crooked and misshapen. Mr. Cordon came over to Rodney's side.

"What do you think?" the teacher asked. "Do you want to re-measure those legs to see if we can't get it level?"

"Well, if you think that will help, I'm willing to give it a try. But it didn't help last week."

"I know," sighed the teacher, his long black hair pulled into a loose ponytail behind his head. "But we can't give up, can we?"

Mr. Cordon's question wasn't rhetorical. A big part of him was hoping that Rodney would just give up. He was even willing to give Rodney a D for effort if he would just stop screwing everything up. This semester alone, the kid had ruined his tile saw, a hammer, and a miter box.

"No, we can't!" said Rodney with enthusiasm as he opened the tape measure, pulled the tape out three feet to begin measuring, and pressed the lever to secure the metal tape. As he let the end go, Rodney realized he hadn't pressed the lever hard enough. The tape slammed back into its holder, smacking him in the face on its wild ride back in. Mr. Cordon just sighed.

♫♫♫

The bell rang to signal the start of second period at Birmingham High, home of the Patriots. Rodney hurried into a classroom full of long black communal counters and stools. The biology room always smelled faintly of formaldehyde, regardless of whether dissections were taking place. Ms. Stanley was seated at her teacher's desk at the front of the room, reviewing her lesson plan. Rodney noticed a female guardian angel standing behind the middle-aged teacher. Ms. Stanley's glasses slipped down her nose and she pushed them back up with her right index finger squarely placed on the bridge. She stood up, brushed her long, frizzy brown hair off of her shoulders, and walked around to the front of her desk.

"So yesterday we talked about neurons and how they fire throughout the body, sending information from, for example, your fingertips, up your arms, and to your brain in a split second. Meanwhile your eyes and ears are gathering information, triggering more neurons to fire, and sending those packets of information to the brain. Do you all remember that?"

A few members of the class nodded noncommittally while others dozed off or stared out windows. Ms. Stanley smoothed her brown plaid polyester skirt and kept talking. "Well, the cerebral cortex gathers input—those packets of information not unlike an email—from all of these billions of neurons firing all over your body all day and night. The cerebral cortex has to make sense of all those emails, put them all together and construct a summary, or story, to help you navigate this world. It's sort of like the National Security Advisor to the President of the United States. He has to gather reports from various sources: CIA, FBI, foreign governments, National Security Council, and then advise the President. He has to make sense of tons of information coming at him every minute. He has to put it all together into a believable narrative. Your cerebral cortex does the same thing. Your ears hear a booming noise, your eyes see a bright light, your nose detects rainwater, your skin feels a strong wind, your cerebral cortex shouts 'thunderstorm!' Get it?"

A few heads in the front row nodded. Rodney half-heartedly paid attention. He wasn't ignoring his teacher but his attention wasn't completely focused on her either. Not until she got to this part.

"Don't forget the brain has two halves. One half spends most of its time receiving info from the neurons. The other half is where the National Security Advisor sits. He doesn't always know where his information is coming from, he just has to make sense of it. Some really interesting studies have been done on people absorbing information they can't explain. They actually make up reasons to explain it."

This got Rodney thinking about the possibility that our brains can lie to us. It was an entirely new thought for him. He had always considered his gray matter a bit slow, but honest. This news disturbed him.

His teacher continued, "Certain essential brain chemicals like dopamine and serotonin grease the wheels of this system. More than that, they really open and close doors for the National Security Advisor, guiding him down some paths, or hallways if you will, and not others. They affect what information he gets and therefore what story he tells. You understand what I'm saying? Your brain chemicals can actually affect your personality by turning up some emotions and dulling others. We've already talked about how testosterone does this to teenage boys and bodybuilders. Remember 'roid rage? And remember how we talked about crying pregnant women? All that emotion comes from the influence of brain chemicals. Well today we're going to talk about how dopamine affects whether or not you believe in God."

Now Ms. Stanley had Rodney's full attention. He raised his hand. "A brain chemical can make me believe in God? Is that what you're saying?" he asked. "How can that be?" He felt as though his peace of mind had just run headlong into an electrified fence.

"Well, studies have been done in England by Peter Brugger and Christine Mohr at the University of Bristol which show a correlation between people with high levels of dopamine and people who believe in ghosts, ESP, conspiracy theories, and God. Dopamine injections led to people finding patterns in random arrangements of dots—we call that patternicity. Those same people also attached meaning to patterns. We call that belief in a higher power or outside agent."

Rodney raised his hand again. "Do you mean that people who believe in God only have faith because they have a lot of dopa-something in their brains?"

∫∫∫

Rodney was having an eye-opening morning. He hadn't seen Satan yet, but already his faith was being challenged. And it was only 8:45 a.m. What's worse, he found his faith being shaken by a Christian biology teacher. He knew she was a believer because he could see her guardian angel. But she was saying things that shook Rodney's faith to his foundation. She was saying that belief originated in the brain and was fueled by a brain chemical called dopamine. He felt that his faith came from his spirit and connected with God. He had never heard anything like this before. He didn't know whether to trust her or not.

Ms. Stanley answered Rodney's question about whether or not it was just dopamine that led to faith in God. "Well, no. There are a lot of factors that lead to belief in God. And high dopamine levels don't guarantee belief in God. Like I said, people with lots of dopamine flowing through their brains might believe in psychics or ghosts or even that the Holocaust never happened. People with high dopamine levels are just more prone to believing what they hear without being skeptical of the sources."

Sharise, the Christian girl from Rodney's Physics class, raised her hand. "Is it fair to say that Christians as a group are more gullible than non-Christians?"

"Yes, it is probably fair to make that generalization, but we all know that generalizations lead to racism and bigotry and hatred. So be careful. Not every Christian is gullible. And not every atheist is a skeptic. Some atheists practice a form of belief that requires just as many leaps of faith as their Christian counterparts. Even scientists are prone to holding beliefs that they can't prove. Have you talked about the theories of multiple universes in physics class? That's a theory with zero proof that is very difficult to swallow without serious faith and probably high dopamine levels. Look, we are a believing species. Some of us believe more easily and rapidly than others."

The bell rang to signal the end of class. Rodney was really upset by what the teacher had just lectured about, so he made his way to her desk.

"Ms. Stanley, do you mind if we talk more about this later? I'm really confused by what you just told us."

Ms. Stanley was thrilled that a student actually wanted more of her tutelage. "Can you come back here on your lunch hour?" she asked. She didn't want to wait until after school.

"Yeah, thanks. I'll be by around 11:30 a.m."

When Rodney returned to the biology classroom an hour and a half later, Ms. Stanley had two halves of an egg-salad sandwich waiting on her desk. She pushed one half toward Rodney.

"Oh, thanks. That's really nice of you. I, um, lent my lunch money to someone else today."

"It's egg salad. I hope you like it. I added some turmeric to the mayo because it's a great anti-inflammatory. I don't want to develop Alzheimer's disease."

"Is that why it's such a bright yellow color?" He took a bite. "It's good. I like it."

"I'm glad. Why don't you tell me what's bothering you?"

"I've always been taught that faith in God comes from God. Now you're teaching that it comes from the brain and hormones. That upsets me."

"Well it shouldn't. There is no real contradiction there. Imagine for a minute that you're God. You've created this species. Wouldn't you want your created beings to be able to perceive you?"

"I guess," said Rodney with a bit of egg salad dangling off the corner of his mouth. "I guess if I didn't, they couldn't worship me. Like the animals—they are created by God, but they don't worship Him."

"Right! It doesn't seem as though animals can perceive God. But humans can. Our brains have to be different in order to do that. In order to perceive our creator, we have to be aware of an agent outside of ourselves. And we have to be able to see His work in our lives. We have to be able to detect patterns, and assign meaning to those patterns. God uses our physical bodies—our brains, our hormones, our neurons—to make Himself known to us."

"Why doesn't He just use supernatural stuff? Why not make more miracles?"

"Well, again, pretend you're God. You've created all the natural laws that govern the universe. They work pretty darn well. Those natural laws get planets and stars created. Those laws keep us alive and multiplying fruitfully. Those laws are pretty perfect. Why would you want to upend them all the time? What would be the point?"

"Well, I guess the point would be that we would believe in Him."

"Jesus performed a lot of miracles. Not everyone who saw them believed He was the Messiah."

"Yeah, I guess that's true."

"The laws of the universe, the study of biology—these things don't contradict God, Rodney. You don't have to feel threatened by science. Often, the study of God's creation just points right back to Him. Astronomy shows us how big He is. Quantum mechanics shows us how organized He is. Psychology shows us how wise He is: how all human behavior has been explained in the Bible and how following God's rules truly is the only path to happiness. God revealed science to us. I'm sure He wants us to use it. For instance, when you get hurt, which seems to happen quite a bit, you go to the hospital and you also pray to get better, right?"

"Oh, yeah! I do."

"You're availing yourself of science and technology. At the same time, you're acknowledging that your creator has the ultimate power over the natural laws He set in motion. And you also are showing that you understand He loves you and cares about your wellbeing. You're using science and faith together, harmoniously. They don't have to be in conflict with each other."

Ms. Stanley's certainty was as calming to Rodney as a 20-pound blanket. "I see what you mean," he said. "So why are so many scientists trying to disprove the existence of God?"

"Well, like I said in class, atheism can become a form of religious belief. Many scientists lean more toward skepticism than belief or are uncomfortable with belief, so they lean too hard away from it. Most reasonable scientists will admit that science in no way cancels out God's presence."

"Shwew! That's a relief. Because I don't want to have to ignore science in order to keep my faith."

"Please don't."

"Thanks, Ms. Stanley. I really needed that."

"You're welcome, Rodney. Now you better hop to your next class."

♫♫♫

It was late on Wednesday night at the Simplessohn household. Rodney, upstairs in his room, was full from dinner and happy that he wasn't fasting anymore, but nervous that his demon pal hadn't visited him yet today. Rodney knew that this was day two of seven days of temptation from a demon who looked like a handsome British actor. This delay was freaking him out.

"Hey Bazooka," Rodney called to his guardian angel who was at that moment standing just behind him. Rodney turned around in his desk chair. "Why isn't Jude Law here yet? Is he playing mind games with me? Because the waiting is killing me. I can't concentrate. Does this demon need only five minutes to make me sin today? Is that it? I'm such a loser."

"I assure you, the demon's plans have been laid. And the Holy Spirit has countered with an urge to read 1 Corinthians, chapter six."

"K, let's see." Rodney grabbed his Bible and began flipping through it. "Here it is, chapter six. Which verse?"

"Twelve."

"I got it. 'All things are lawful for me, but all things are not helpful. All things are lawful for me, but I will not be brought under the power of any.' What does that mean?"

"All things are legal for you, since you are not under the old testament law, thanks to Jesus. But that doesn't mean that no consequences come from sinning. That doesn't mean that you should submit to your bodily desires. Obtaining freedom from the flesh is the reason some people fast. Overcoming hunger leads to overcoming other fleshly impulses. It strengthens the will. Remember: spirits are greater than bodies. Read on, lad, read on."

Rodney continued, "'Now the body is not for sexual immorality but for the Lord.' I don't like where this is going." He looked up at Barook. "Is Jude Law going to try to tempt me with the ladies?"

"Count on it. It's as certain as your love of cupcakes."

"Oh boy." Rodney looked back down at his Bible. "What else does it say? 'Flee sexual immorality. Every sin that a man does is outside the body, but he who commits sexual immorality sins against his own body. Or do you not know that your body is the temple of the Holy Spirit who is in you, whom you have from God, and you are not your own? For you were bought at a price; therefore, glorify God in your body and in your spirit, which are God's.' That's some heavy stuff."

"Yes, heavy—" Barook was interrupted by the sudden appearance of Satan flying through Rodney's bedroom window.

"Yikes!" yelled Rodney at the surprise visitor wearing a black Armani suit with a tiny purple pinstripe. "Knock next time, dude. That's kinda rude."

"So sorry, my dear man. Won't happen again. Shall I go out and re-enter?" Satan sweetly asked in his upper-class British accent. His dashing smile and blond hair made him seem so sophisticated and harmless, as did his pastel purple shirt and silk tie.

"Nah, don't worry about it," Rodney said. "What do you want?"

"Is that any way to greet a being who's been so attentive to you?"

"Sorry, Jude. I'm just a little uptight over this whole temptation thing."

"Rodney, Rodney, Rodney. You need to relax. We're just hanging out together for a few days. It's nothing to be afraid of."

"Are you gonna tempt me with sex?"

"I promise you, I will never ever tempt you into my bed. I do not find you particularly attractive, young man."

"No, I mean, are you gonna try to get me to have sex before I'm married?"

"Why? Would you like me to? Every hot-blooded American boy wants to be with a limber young lady. Why look, if I just surf the web for a second," Satan bent over Rodney's shoulder, materialized his hands for a moment, and began typing on the keyboard of his laptop. "V*oila!*"

Rodney leaned over to look at what Satan had dialed up. It was pictures of beautiful women wearing nothing but a smile and the occasional cowboy hat.

"Oh boy," said Rodney. "They're gorgeous, but I can't."

"It's not sexual immorality," purred Jude Law. "You aren't even touching them. That's not a sin."

"Sin in the mind equals sin in the flesh," said Barook.

"I can't look at that stuff with Bazooka standing right here," said Rodney.

"Well, Bazooka will turn his back, won't you my good man?"

"Nay, not I."

"Oh, you're such a bloody git," sneered Satan at Barook.

"I am aware," said Barook.

"C'mon Rodney, let's get out of here. I know a cool place we can hang out together."

Rodney looked to Barook for a clue as to whether to go with Satan or not. Barook nodded. He knew that Satan could whisk Rodney away to anywhere in the world with a touch of his demonic hand. He didn't think Rodney was ready for that kind of travel just yet. He might come unglued. Barook calculated that if Rodney went willingly with Satan right now, Satan probably wouldn't work his evil transporting magic just yet.

Rodney didn't want his parents to know that he was going out so late at night. And he really didn't want to explain to them that he was heading somewhere unknown with a creature from hell. He chose to climb out his window, onto the tree that grew beside it, and down to the lawn at the side of the house, instead. Barook flew just behind him. Rodney began walking toward his Pacer when Jude Law cleared his throat. "I thought we'd travel in style tonight. I took the liberty of hiring a car." Satan stretched his graceful arm toward the curb where a black limousine was parked.

"Epic," said Rodney as he wandered over to the stretched-out Lincoln. The driver jumped out of the front seat and quickly opened the back door for Rodney. "Thanks, man," he said to the tall guy in the cap.

"Tell him to take us to the Wiltern," Satan whispered to Rodney as they settled into the back seat with Barook.

"Where to?" asked the driver after he was back behind the steering wheel.

"Um, the Wiltern Theatre."

"In Koreatown?"

"Yeah, sure," said Rodney eyeing Satan for confirmation.

"Check your back pocket," said Jude Law with a sly smile.

"Tickets to the Dandy Warhols concert tonight? That's fire!" the teen beamed with excitement. Barook had a feeling he knew what Satan was up to.

∯∯

Courtney Taylor-Taylor was up on the dark stage of the Art-Deco Wiltern Theatre in L.A.'s Koreatown, near downtown. He was strumming his guitar and belting out soulful lyrics begging his girlfriend to embrace his life of leisure and alcohol on the road. To his right, keyboardist Zia McCabe was playing the keys and gyrating to the melody. Rodney couldn't take his eyes off of her thin T-shirt.

Rodney was packed into the standing crowd at the front of the stage, swaying along with other fans and trying not to inhale the thick smoke coming from fat, hand-rolled cigarettes being passed around. He loved the way the drums pounded through his chest and reverberated off of his bones. Cute girls with tattoos and facial piercings were scattered amongst the hipster guys in jeans and T-shirts sporting thick mustaches and beards. Rodney felt cool for once in his life. He pulled out his phone and live-streamed a few minutes of the concert. He couldn't wait to tell Kim about this tomorrow morning on the way to school.

"Let's go get a drink" shouted Jude Law into Rodney's ear. "The bar is just outside in the lobby."

"Why? I'm having fun right here!" Rodney yelled back to no one visible.

"We need to work on your pick-up skills," said the demon, hoping a real live girl would be able to coax Rodney into full-blown lust and maybe even into fornication. This demon had no idea what a dork he was dealing with.

Satan managed to lure Rodney out of the jam-packed crowd and into a less-full lobby scattered with pub tables. Video screens showed the concert happening on stage and the band's music was being piped out here, too. Jude led Rodney to a table full of girls. Rodney introduced himself with, "Hey ladies. How's it hanging?" He sounded as oily as a DJ on the Jersey shore.

The girls rolled their eyes and looked away while Jude whispered, "Offer them a ride in your limo out front."

"Who wants to take a ride with me?" barked Rodney.

"No, you have to mention the limo or the girls will imagine a white van with no windows," Jude Law tried to explain.

A pretty pink-haired girl with a stud through her eyebrow, fished in her purse for something while saying to her companions, "We are not gonna get kidnapped tonight ladies. Leave it to me."

She pulled out a small metal canister, smiled, and shot Rodney full in the face with pepper spray.

"Arrggggggggghhhhhhhhhhhhhhh!" he screamed and dropped to the ground, clutching his eyes.

"See! No more stranger danger," she beamed while the girls with her laughed in relief.

"Oh well that went well," sneered Satan at Rodney. "You are definitely not going to be fornicating tonight."

Barook swept some wet napkins off the table onto Rodney who was writhing just below it. "Use these to wipe your eyes," he offered.

Adoram flew in at that moment. Seeing the two angels and the three girls staring at Rodney on the ground pawing at his eyes with the wet napkins, he asked, "What's going on here?"

"The demon loses to the dork tonight," answered the guardian angel.

"Oh, well, that's wonderful," responded the seraph. "Does Rodney need something? He looks uncomfortable."

"Time. He needs time to heal his wounded pride. I'll see him home safely, sir," said Barook.

"I hate this kid," muttered Satan, walking away from the scene of his crushing defeat.

"Ah, well," said Adoram looking down at Rodney. "I suppose we're done here." To Barook he added, "I'll see you both tomorrow."

Chapter 8

*The patient in spirit is better than
the proud in spirit.*

~ Ecclesiastes 7:8

Rodney was tired in his shop class the next morning. It was 8 a.m. He had been out too late at the Dandy Warhols concert the night before with Satan. His eyes were still red and irritated from the pepper spray. He couldn't see too well. He was fumbling around with his three-legged table, trying to make it not so crooked.

Rodney took his table over to the circular saw. He wanted to trim one of the legs he had marked yesterday. His guardian angel, Barook, looked on with concern. Not liking where things were going, Barook flew over to the teacher, Mr. Cordon, who was helping a student with his birdhouse. Barook clapped his hands in front of Brett's eyes hoping to get his attention. Actions and emotions in the spiritual world can sometimes bleed through dimensions and make their way into human consciousness. Mr. Cordon looked up in time to see Rodney turn on the circular saw and place his table leg, with his fingers still wrapped around it, in the path of the spinning saw.

"Hold on there a sec, Rodney. Maybe you wanna check your hand placement?"

"Nah, I'm good," said Rodney who was about to perform an amputation on himself.

"George," said Mr. Cordon to the boy with the birdhouse, "is Rodney good?"

"No, Mr. Cordon," said George. "He's going to saw his fingers off, which will be epic to watch, actually. Do we really have to stop him? I'm pretty sure the blood will spurt everywhere."

At that Rodney jumped back away from the saw with a look of horror on his face. He let go of the stool and it clattered to the floor and broke apart. "Maybe I need some coffee," Rodney muttered.

"Why don't you take a break and run to the cafeteria?" offered Mr. Cordon who was thinking about all the paperwork another accident would trigger. He filled out a hall pass and handed it to Rodney.

"That's really nice of you. Thanks," said Rodney on his way out the door. In the mostly empty hallway Rodney noticed a group of three polo-shirted guys wearing Cartier wristwatches and Sperry boat shoes. Rodney looked down at his cheap Target-brand loafers made of pleather that were too tight for his feet.

"Man, it would be nice to be able to afford better things," Rodney said to his angelic companion.

"Of course it would," said Barook.

Rodney squinted and turned his head slowly in Barook's direction. "That's not very comforting," he blurted out a little too loudly for someone who appeared to be walking by himself.

The group of wealthy guys looked over at Rodney. "What's not very comforting?" one of them asked.

"Um, my underwear" stammered Rodney, turning red.

"I think you're over-sharing, bra" said one of the teens.

"Yeah, probably," muttered Rodney as he passed the group on his way to the cafeteria and some much-needed awake juice.

ʃʃʃʃ

Rodney was sitting in Mr. Thaxton's physics class staring at Selefina. He was thinking about how beautiful she was. Her dark hair was quite silky. Rodney thought it looked like midnight in Costa Rica. Not that he had ever been to Costa Rica. But he had heard stuff. And he was feeling poetic. He gazed at her green eyes. He thought about envy. "No wait—that's not good," he said to himself. So he compared them in his mind to emeralds.

Barook looked at Rodney mooning over Selefina and began to worry, just a little. He couldn't read Rodney's thoughts, but he could read that stupid look on Rodney's face. And he trusted Selefina about as much as he trusted a pregnant alligator.

Selefina turned her head and caught Rodney staring at her. She smiled at him. "Do you want to give me your lunch money again, today?" she asked sweetly.

"Um, yeah," said Rodney fumbling for his wallet. He wanted to give her lots of things, pretty things, expensive things. She took the money out of his hand as the bell rang. Once again, the demon snake that was coiled around her body extended its neck and bit Rodney. This time he didn't recoil. He was getting used to this. He almost liked it now.

Rodney walked out of physics class, following a few steps behind Selefina on his way to the cafeteria. He stared dreamily at the back of her head and elegantly swaying shoulders as she moved through the crowded hallways.

"Hey, hot dog!" shouted Kim as Rodney entered the cafeteria.

"Hey, pork butt!" Rodney shot back.

"Oh! Nice one!" responded Kim. "You're on your game today. Good to have you back."

"Ya got any money I can borrow?'

"Sure. What happened to yours?" said Kim, handing Rodney enough to buy lunch for the day as they got in line for the food.

"I gave it to Selefina. It sure would be nice to not be so poor."

"Poor? You're not poor. You live in a two-story house with only two other people. You don't have to work. You own a car. And a computer. And a cell phone. By the standards of any third-world country, you live a wealthy, pampered existence."

Rodney pouted. His gaze wandered over to Selefina across the room. "My car isn't going to impress anyone. I don't have enough cash to take a girl out to dinner."

Kim followed Rodney's stare. "Oh, I see what this is about. I think you just need a little perspective. Hey Elias!" Kim waved at their friend from English Lit who was already sitting down eating his sandwich.

Elias waved them over. After they got their food, Rodney and Kim set their trays down next to him and settled into their seats. "Hey guys, what's happening?" Elias asked.

"We haven't hung out in a while," said Kim. "Do you mind if we come over to your place after school?"

"No problem. I have to be at work at 5 p.m., so I have a little time before that."

"Rodney can give you a ride home, right?" Kim said while nudging Rodney with his elbow.

"Oh yeah, sure. Just meet us in the parking lot," said Rodney.

Kim showed Elias the live-stream of the Dandy Warhols concert that Rodney had made last night.

Rodney whispered to no one visible, "My clothes are lame," and "Do girls notice haircuts?"

∬∬

Rodney and Kim were driving to Elias' house after school. Elias was in the back seat. The guardian angels assigned to Rodney and Kim had chosen to fly just above the Pacer without Rodney's objection. They were joined by Elnathan, Elias' guardian. The second back seat was taken up by a spirit being who was the spitting image of Jude Law. Since the devil had permission from God to tempt Rodney, the dominion angels just kept an eye on him instead of trying to do battle with him.

Rodney pulled up in front of the Rodriguez household and parked on the street. The small driveway was completely taken up by a huge recreational vehicle. "Nice RV," said Rodney while holding the seat forward and helping Elias out of the back of his tiny car. "Do you take many trips in it?"

"No," said Elias. "My Uncle Diego and his family live in there."

"Oh," said Rodney. "I thought your uncle and his family lived inside your house with you."

"That's Uncle Geronimo," corrected Elias.

"Oh, I see," said Rodney, following Elias and Kim toward the front door, stepping around all the children's toys strewn across the front lawn. Then he turned his head over his shoulder and whispered to the air, "That's rude! Why are you so mean?"

As Elias opened the front door, a cute brown-haired mutt bounded out barking excitedly to greet his master. "Hey, Yelp. Say 'hi' to the guys," Elias told his dog. Rodney ran his fingers through the dog's soft coat. Yelp began barking at something next to Rodney that Elias couldn't see.

"Yelp, stop it," said Elias. "Come on in, everyone."

"Ugh, it's so crowded around here," Jude Law said with a pout on his face, following Rodney across the threshold. "And dirty. Being poor is so horrible. Is there anything worse?"

Two children ran screaming and laughing through the tidy living room as the boys walked through it the other way toward the kitchen. Mrs. Rodriguez shouted to her son from the small adjoining dining room, "Elias, don't forget that you have the computer tonight from 10-11 p.m. Sorry it's so late, but Pedro has a paper due tomorrow and he needs it more than you."

"Yes, *Madre*. I remember," said Elias. "It's no problem. Are you home from work?" he asked, wandering over to her side. She was seated at the dining room table, paying a stack of bills.

"Only for a little while, *cariño*," said his mom, kissing the back of his hand. "You boys want some horchata? I just made a fresh batch."

"Oh yes, please!" said Kim excitedly. He loved her cinnamon-rice milk. "Help yourself," she motioned to the kitchen.

Elias filled three plastic cups with the sweet, refreshing drink and handed two of them over to his friends. As they all wandered out into the mostly dirt-covered back yard hemmed in by a chain-link fence, Kim offered, "You know, Elias, I have an old laptop that I'm not using. I just got a new one with the money I made from my web-design work. You wanna use it? It's just sitting around."

"Are you sure?" asked Elias, his face lighting up. "That would be great! Thanks, man! God is really good to me."

Elias arranged a few rusty metal beach chairs in a semicircle in the dirt, kicked some toy dump trucks out of the way, and sat down. Kim took the middle chair and Rodney took the chair on the far right. Jude Law stood next to him, a look of disgust on his face. "Money would make this place so much better. Money solves a lot of problems. Too bad God chose not to bless this family."

"You think?" Rodney asked, turning his head to the right.

"Thanks for having us over. It's a nice place," Kim said quickly, in an attempt to distract Elias from Rodney's odd behavior.

"No, it isn't," said Elias frankly. "But it's all we can afford. And it's so much better than the houses my relatives own in Mexico. We have reliable electricity. The walls are insulated. We have indoor plumbing. We are well and truly blessed. We live in this country legally, so we don't have to fear the police. We don't have to bribe any government officials to get by like my uncles in Mexico do. We are all healthy here. We have enough money to buy medicine. Yes, we have to share a lot. No, I don't have much privacy. But we love each other. We are nice to each other. We have a good life and I'm grateful to God for it. I will even be able to go to college as long as I keep working at night. And then I will have the chance to make an even better life for all of us."

"You have a great attitude and that's worth more than gold. And a great family. Money can't buy those things," said Kim, attempting to teach Rodney a valuable life lesson. As Elias was nodding in agreement, Rodney blurted out, "Yeah, but money can really help! Wouldn't you want to win the lottery?"

"Sure!" said Elias. "Wouldn't you?"

"Heck yeah! I would buy all sorts of nice things: a new car, fancy clothes, jewelry for my girl."

"What girl?" asked Elias as Kim's eyes grew wide and he almost spit out his horchata.

Rodney answered, "Well, she's not my girl yet. But Selefina has fine taste. And if I could buy her nice things, I bet she would be my girl soon."

"Selefina?" asked Elias, wrinkling up his nose. "You like her? She's pretty, but she's super shallow."

"I don't mind that," said Rodney. Kim rolled his eyes at this. Yelp wandered over and stood next to Rodney, staring at the air beside him.

Elias shrugged and said, "I figured you for better taste in ladies, but I guess the heart has its own mind."

"It does," said Rodney smiling. Yelp lifted his leg and peed, seemingly onto thin air. Rodney turned his head to see what the dog was doing and started laughing hysterically.

Before Elias could ask what was so funny, Kim hit Rodney on the arm and asked, "Doesn't she remind you of Daisy in *The Great Gatsby*?" Rodney looked confused at the question, so Kim elaborated. "You know, the book we're halfway through reading in English Lit?"

"Oh, I haven't started reading that yet," admitted Rodney. Kim shook his head and now it was Elias' turn to LOL.

As Elias went back into the house to refill their drinks, Rodney turned to Satan and said, "Look, if you're going to spend the whole hour trying to convince me that money is important, you might as well leave now. I agree with you. I mean, it doesn't seem to bother Elias to not have any, but I'm gonna need some serious income in order to have a good life."

"It seems my work here is done for the day," said Jude Law, shaking his wet pant leg and disappearing.

"Do you really believe that?" asked Kim.

"I don't know. But demons can't read my thoughts, so it doesn't really matter. It got him to go away."

"Well, I hope you get over your money hunger soon. Dissatisfaction can lead to misery. Be careful what you believe." Turning his head over his shoulder to look at Elias laughing with his nieces and nephews, Kim said, "I think Elias will be happy his whole life."

∫∫∫∫

"Rodney, come help me stir the broccolini!" yelled Sheryl Simplessohn from the kitchen of her home. Her son bounded down the stairs from his room to where his mom was standing in front of the stove.

"I'm here. Whaddya need?" he asked.

"Here," she said, handing him a silicon spatula. "Keep the broccolini moving in the sauté pan while I open the release valve on the pressure cooker. Stand back. The steam will be coming out of here pretty fast." Barook moved between Rodney and the pressure cooker, just in case.

"What are we having?"

"Sloppy Joe's with those bitter green vegetables you are stirring on the side," she said as the pressure cooker hissed and sputtered, sending clouds of steam up to the ceiling.

Rodney wrinkled up his nose. "Can I put some butter on this baby broccoli?"

"Well, it's got olive oil on it already. Have you tried it?" she asked. Rodney grabbed a chopped-up piece of the good-for-you veggie out of the pan and threw it into his mouth."

"Owwww! Hot! Hot!" he screamed while trying to chew it. Eventually he swallowed as his mom shook her head. Barook ran his hands down his face. Even though he had been keeping Rodney safe from catastrophic harm for all of the boy's 18 years, the guardian angel was still amazed at Rodney's capacity to hurt himself. Sheba, Sheryl's guardian angel, just smiled and shrugged her shoulders at Barook as if to say, "I'm glad he's not my problem."

"Yeah, it needs butter," Rodney eventually said.

"Go ahead," Sheryl sighed. "But don't blame me when your cholesterol gets high. I've done everything I could."

While Rodney rooted around in the refrigerator for some butter, Sheryl yelled out to her husband, "David! Come set the table!"

"Set it where?" he asked, laughing at his own corny joke. Nimrod, his guardian, laughed, too. Rodney and his mom exchanged a look that said, "Oh, brother."

Thirty minutes later Rodney was stuffed and his mom began clearing the table. "Hey dad," Rodney ventured.

"Yes?"

"How did you get mom to fall in love with you?"

Sheryl, overhearing this from the kitchen, decided to give her boys some privacy. Although she was insanely curious, she kept herself from going back into the dining room by washing the dishes, even though it was David's job.

"What? Where is this coming from? Is there a girl you're trying to impress?"

"Well, yeah. She's in my physics class. But she likes really nice things. My car won't impress her. I can't buy her jewelry or take her anywhere fancy. How am I ever supposed to find a wife without being rich?"

"Well, I hate to say it Rodney, but if you want a girl who needs money to be happy, you're pretty sure to be unhappy. Money spends fast. And when it runs out, which it usually does, she will run out right behind it. I'm not saying you won't be successful one day. But odds are you will end up in the middle class where we are now. Where most people are. And you will probably work for a standard jerk of a boss. And you will feel trapped by your mortgage and car payments. And some nights you will lie awake because you don't know how you're going to pay for your child's college education."

"For crying out loud, dad! That's awful! Why are you telling me this?"

"I'm not trying to scare you or depress you, but I feel like you deserve to know the truth. I want you to have realistic expectations of life, and make good choices based on that. Right now it seems like you have all the potential in the world to be wealthy or have some amazing job that you love. And I hope that you achieve those things. I really do. But most of us don't. Most of us end up a little disillusioned with life and a little disappointed in ourselves."

"Dad, that's horrible!"

"Well, no it isn't. It isn't horrible because money, power, and success aren't what matter. You shouldn't be seeking glory for yourself in the first place. I mean, don't get me wrong, it's only natural to do so. And you'll probably have to learn this lesson for yourself the hard way. But your ultimate goal in life should be to seek glory for God. Because if you are seeking glory for yourself, you will likely be disappointed in yourself. And in order to be disappointed in yourself, you must have trusted in yourself. And that means you put your trust in the wrong place, son. I know because I've been there."

David got up from the table and grabbed the Bible laying on the sideboard behind him. He sat back down and opened it to where his bookmark lay. Flipping back a few pages he said, "I'm reading Jeremiah right now. You might find a couple of the verses in it helpful. David showed Rodney Jeremiah 17:7-8. He read out loud, "'Blessed is the man who trusts in the Lord, and whose hope is the Lord. For he shall be like a tree planted by the waters which spreads out its roots by the river, and will not fear when the heat comes; but its leaf will be green, and will not be anxious in the year of drought nor will cease from yielding fruit.' You see?"

"I would sure like to be able to trust in the Lord more," answered Rodney. "Lately I'm full of anxieties and fear. And I don't think I've ever yielded any fruit."

"Oh, you yield the fruit of joy for me every day, son," said David smiling. "Don't worry. The truth is, God loves working through seemingly unimportant people: the unremarkable, the humble, the flawed, the poor, and the foolish. Let His strength, His wisdom, His power, His spirit flow through you. Focus on Him, not on yourself. And if you want to trust God more, read this." With that he flipped some more Bible pages back and showed Rodney Jeremiah 9:23-24.

Rodney read aloud, "'Let not the wise man glory in his wisdom, let not the mighty man glory in his might, nor let the rich man glory in his riches, but let him who glories, glory in this. That he understands and knows Me, that I am the Lord, exercising lovingkindness, judgement, and righteousness in the earth. For in these I delight says the Lord.' Wow. I guess I just need to know the Lord more in order to be able to trust Him more."

"Bingo."

"And that will help me be like a tree?"

"Right."

"Do girls like trees?"

"Well, in the sense that a tree is a stable man who trusts in God, yes. Your mom did."

"Really? That's how you got mom?"

"That, and my wicked sense of humor." At this Nimrod nodded vigorously. Rodney cast a glace over his dad's shoulder at Nimrod and said, "Well, I know it wasn't your jokes. Those are stupid. So, it must have been your trust in God. That's good to know."

"Remember, a woman should love you for who you are, not for what you can buy her."

"Thanks, dad. I better go do my homework now."

∫∫∫∫

Tricklane, Satan's right-hand demon, sat in the tree outside Rodney's bedroom window. Scumbert, the demon frog who discovered Rodney's super power, was next to him on a big branch.

"I don't smell fear on him," Tricklane concluded.

"Ribbit," croaked Scumbert.

"He's in a good place. We need to knock him out of there. We need to remind him that he's still under the curse of the law."

"But he isn't under the curse of the law. He's under the new covenant of grace which—" Scumbert was silenced by Tricklane's demon hand.

"Shut up! He doesn't have a good grasp on that. Most Christians don't. We'll bring him face to face with the law and all the ways he's fallen short of it, and his faith will fizzle. It works every time."

Inside the room, Rodney was on his laptop checking his Instagram account. He scrolled across a photo of Selefina in a sexy red dress. She had posted it 30 minutes ago. In the comments, she wrote, "Don't I look good in this Rodney?"

"Hey Bazooka, look at this!" Rodney screamed. "Selefina tagged me in one of her posts! That's fire!"

"Is it?" asked Barook.

"Oh, yeah!" replied the beaming red-head. "What should I say?" He typed "Yaaasss!" as a reply, then wrinkled up his face. "That's cringy, isn't it? Why did I send that? It makes me look so thirsty."

"Ribbit—Rick is not going to like this," said Scumbert.

"What does that have to do with condemnation?" snapped Tricklane.

"Nothing. It has more to do with—croak—secret love and teen angst."

"Oh, well then, we might have to change course. I see a better way to effectuate my plan," said the fallen angel in the tree. "We need to get over to Rick's place, right now."

"This—crooaaakk—way," replied Scumbert as he hopped down from the tree branch to the ground.

Ricardo Oscar Gutierrez was a star soccer player at Birmingham Community Charter High School. He was in Rodney's physics class, but Rodney never really noticed him there. Rick never really noticed Rodney either. They were both too busy staring at Selefina from 10:08 to 11:36 every weekday morning. But tonight, Rick would suddenly learn who Rodney was.

Tricklane, with Scumbert perched on his shoulder, flew into Rick's bedroom. He landed by Rick's ear and whispered, "Check Instagram."

Rick was sitting in bed, typing a term paper on his laptop. He suddenly felt the urge to take a break and picked up his phone. He tapped on his Instagram app to see what his friends were up to. He noticed a photo of Selefina in his feed. He clicked on the post and was admiring how she looked when he saw that she had tagged some doofus named Rodney. "Who the heck is Rodney?" he asked himself out loud. Rick clicked on the hyperlink which took him to Rodney's page. "What a dork!" he laughed. Tricklane, still snuggled up to Rick's ear, spoke into it: "What if she likes him?"

"She can't be into him!" Rick yelled to no one in particular.

"What if this guy is your competition?"

"This isn't happening!"

"What are you going to do about it?"

Rick clenched his teeth and said, "I need to do something about this."

Tricklane smiled. "It works every time," he said to Scumbert.

Chapter 9

*Rest in the Lord and wait patiently for Him; Do not fret
because of him who prospers in his way. Because of the man
who brings wicked schemes to pass. Cease from anger and
forsake wrath;
Do not fret—it only causes harm.*

~ Psalms 37:7-8

It was Friday morning. The Santa Anas were blowing. Rodney hated the Santa Anas. Normally the wind blew cool and clean off the Pacific Ocean onto the shore, freshening his stale bedroom 30 miles inland. But today, the wind blew hot and dry off the Santa Ana mountain range, dragging with it dust, dirt, pollen, yeast, and the graphite that fell out of airplane engines as jet fuel burned. Its lack of moisture amped up the static electricity in the air, giving him a nasty shock every time he touched a light switch, his car door handle, or anything at all metal, no matter how thick the rubber on his soles. He hated the Santa Anas. They brought nothing good.

Rodney filed into his physics class just as the bell was ringing. On the way in he bumped into a muscular guy with short dark hair wearing nylon shorts that reached below his knees. "Sorry, man" said Rodney.

Rick turned to look at who knocked into him and his eyes widened. He recognized Rodney from Selefina's post last night. Rick didn't say anything back to Rodney; he just glared. Rodney didn't have time to think about the glare. Mr. Thaxton was already starting his lecture as Rodney scrambled to take his seat, open his notebook, and start taking notes.

Selefina, on the other hand, did have time to notice the interaction between Rodney and the guy she liked. She had been trying to get Rick to notice her for weeks. She had batted her eyelashes, asked him for favors, touched his arm as often as she could, but got barely two words in return. She had no idea how shy Rick really was, or that he was desperately in love with her, but terrified to speak to her. Most guys were much more overt in their affections. Boys she had never spoken to before asked her out on dates and proposed marriage. Not Rick. He would barely look at her in class.

She was getting desperate. Last night she even tagged that red-headed dorkmeister hoping to make Rick jealous. It might have worked. He really gave Rodney a dirty look on the way in the door. Now his eyes were boring a hole in the back of Rodney's head. It was a good start. She would have to crank up the heat.

Barook, after a thousand years on the job, had the skills and reactions of a Secret Service agent. He also noticed the rage in Rick's eyes. "This is not good," he thought. He placed himself between Rick and Rodney for the hour, just to be safe. He didn't like the smirk on Selefina's face either. Or the big smile on her demon snake. Or the fact that a couple of new demons were in the room. They looked like the dapper guy and the frog who were staring into Rodney's bedroom window last night. Not that Rodney noticed them, then or now. Rodney never seemed alert to danger. He was completely oblivious to everything going on around him. He could be on an airplane, mid-hijack, and buzz the stewardess for a Coke. He just had no clue.

When the bell rang to signal the end of class, Selefina leaned over and touched Rodney's hand. "Do you want my lunch money?" he asked while fishing out his wallet.

"Well, yes," she said, stealing a glance behind her at Rick. She hadn't planned on asking him for the money, but since he was offering, she may as well take it.

The sight of Selefina touching Rodney put Rick over the edge. Tricklane shouted at him, "Are you going to put up with that?" Apparently, Rick wasn't. He jumped out of his chair, ran up to Rodney still seated at his desk, and smacked him on the back of the head. "Hey, jerk!" he hissed. "I don't like being bumped. Meet me in the parking lot after school."

Rodney's head bounced forward and his mouth dropped open. He didn't know what was happening. Selefina's eyes glowed with anticipation. She stared up at Rick from her chair and said, "He drives an ugly orange Pacer. It's round and stupid looking. We'll meet you next to it."

Rick nodded at her and darted out of the classroom before Rodney could close his mouth. "What the heck?" Rodney asked as Selefina grabbed the cash out of his hand.

"He was so salty to you! You really shouldn't disrespect a guy like Rick. He'll kill you," she said. "He's quiet but a raging fire burns within. He may be short, but he's really strong. I'll see you around 4:30 by your car."

"Wait!" Rodney shouted as Selefina gathered her things and sashayed out the door toward the cafeteria, satisfied with the turn of events. She planned to throw herself into Rick's arms after the fight and exclaim, "Oh Rick, that was so macho! How can any girl resist you?" The only reasonable response on his part would be to kiss her. Anyone could see that.

As the classroom was emptying, Rodney looked at Barook and asked, "What just happened?" A blond baseball player answered him, "You're going to get your butt kicked by Rick after school. I don't know what you did, but I sure hope it was worth it."

"I don't know what I did either," said Rodney pathetically.

"Bummer. You know any Judo or Taekwondo?"

"No," said Rodney weakly.

"That's too bad. This is going to be a very uninteresting fight."

"Not for me."

"I guess not, buddy," laughed the jock.

$$\int\int\int$$

In the cafeteria, Rodney was updating Kim and Elias on the recent disaster. Kim noticed Rodney hadn't even touched his tater tots. Rodney loved tater tots. This was serious. Kim was going to need some extra help to sort this one out. Neither he nor Elias had ever been in a fight before. They couldn't even really understand how this fight got started. Rodney was rambling on but not giving them any details that made any sense. Kim scanned the lunchroom. Just then, emerging from the lunch line carrying a tray topped with a burger and crispy potato crowns was Sharise. Sharise wasn't a fighter, but she was wise for her age. Kim pointed her out to Elias. "What do you think? Should we call in reinforcements?" he asked.

"Definitely," said Elias. "We're in over our heads here. I don't even know what Rodney is talking about, much less how to help him."

Kim waved his hands in the air. "Sharise! Do you mind sitting with us today? We need your advice."

Curious, she made her way over to the boys' table and sat down across from them. She looked over at her usual table where her friends were sitting. Viera, the green-eyed girl, threw her hands up in the air and raised her eyebrows as if to say, "What's up?" Sharise made the "one minute" symbol with her hand and turned back to the table where the boys were sitting like three monkeys in a row: hear no evil, see no evil, speak no evil. Except that Rodney could now see all kinds of evil.

"K guys, spill the tea" she commanded as she sat down. Her guardian angel, Sapphire, who looked like a heavy-set black woman with sparkling blue eyes, sat down next to her and nodded at Barook, Koram, and Elnathan standing just behind the boys.

Rodney whined, "I'm going to get killed!" Sapphire shot Barook a questioning look. Barook shook his head.

"What!?" exclaimed Sharise. Sapphire leaned over to her charge and said, "That boy is being dramatic."

"Are you Draking right now?" Sharise asked with narrowed eyes.

"Yes," Kim answered. Behind him Koram nodded.

"Maybe a little," said Rodney. "But you know that soccer player named Rick? I think his last name is Gutierrez or Gonzalez or something."

"Short guy? Dark, curly hair?" asked Sharise.

"That's him," said Rodney. "He wants to kill me. And I have no idea why."

"He has some idea why," said Barook to Sapphire. Sapphire said to Sharise, "There's always a reason why." Sharise answered Rodney with, "There must be some reason. Think. What happened before he said he wanted to kill you?"

"I bumped into him on the way into class."

Barook said to Sapphire, "It's because of Selefina." Sapphire said to Sharise, "What do men always fight about? If it's not money or power, what could it be?"

Sharise thought for a moment and responded to Rodney, "That can't be it. There must be a girl involved somehow. Is there a girl involved?"

"A girl? Well, Selefina was there," said Rodney.

"Bingo," said Sharise. "I knew it. That girl is no good."

"What do you mean?" asked Rodney. "She's so pretty."

"So, you think because a girl is pretty, she has to be good?" shot Sharise. "Is that it? Is that what your stupid man brain really thinks?"

I dunno," said Rodney dejectedly. "When you say it out loud, it sounds really pathetic."

"That's because it is really pathetic," said Sharise. "Have you no sense of character? Have you no clue about women?"

"To be fair," said Kim, trying to save his friend, "he's not around them much. They don't usually let him get near them."

"Oh," said Sharise softening a little as Barook and Sapphire laughed.

"That's so true!" Barook said to Sapphire.

"I think he has something there," Sapphire said to Sharise.

"Maybe I'm being a little hard on you," Sharise said to Rodney.

"Yeah!" said Rodney.

"Rick wants to fight Rodney after school in the parking lot," Kim summarized.

"Hmmm," said Sharise. "Well it seems to me that you need to, well," Sharise's voice trailed off as she turned her head to her right side to think. It was almost as if she knew her guardian angel were there, waiting with some good knowledge to impart.

"Run away?" Rodney asked.

"Beg for mercy?" inquired Kim, attempting to finish Sharise's thought.

"Trust in the Lord," said Sapphire nodding her head.

"Trust that God has this situation in hand," finished Sharise.

"How do I do that?" asked Rodney.

"Sharise whipped out her phone and initiated her Bible app. "I have some verses bookmarked in my YouVersion Bible. Here we go. This is Isaiah 26:3-4: 'You will keep him in perfect peace whose mind is stayed on You, because he trusts in You. Trust in the Lord forever, for in YAHWEH, the Lord, is everlasting strength'."

"She's a spiritual warrior, that girl!" said Sapphire glowing with her usual angel glory and also some pride in her human charge. Barook and Koram nodded in agreement.

"I'm gonna get such a beat down. This is so sucktastic," mumbled Rodney.

Seeing that the verse didn't have the desired effect, Sharise tried again. "How about Proverbs? You like Proverbs 3:5-6? 'Trust in the Lord with all your heart and lean not on your own understanding. In all your ways acknowledge Him and He shall direct your paths.'"

"My path is leading to the parking lot where my beautiful face will be mangled forever," pouted Rodney.

"I dunno about beautiful," Kim whispered to Elias who tried hard not to laugh out loud.

"K," Sharise tried again. "What about Zechariah 4:6? It's a classic. 'Not by might nor by power, but by My Spirit says the Lord of hosts.' How can you not love that one?"

"That's my girl!" exclaimed Sapphire.

Rodney looked directly at Barook and said, "Well, His spirit had better be with me at 4:30 this afternoon. Protecting me. Keeping me from harm. Or I am gonna be really, really mad."

Sharise rolled her eyes. "It's not a bargain. Jesus wants to take care of you because He loves you, not because you are threatening Him."

"I'm not sure I'm worth it, actually," Rodney admitted with his head down.

"Of course you're not," Sharise said gently. "Nobody is. That's the beauty of His love. Listen to this." She read from her phone again. "Romans 8:31-32 says 'What then shall we say to these things? If God is for us, who can be against us? He who did not spare His own Son, but delivered Him up for us all, how shall He not with Him also freely give us all things?' Isn't that great? Just keep repeating that to yourself for the rest of the day. You'll be fine. Now I have to go sit with my girlfriends before they start spreading rumors." Sharise stood up from the table, pushed her chair in, and picked up her tray of food. She nodded goodbye to the guys and headed for her usual table.

"She's so amazing," Elias said as Sharise walked away with Sapphire right behind her. "She categorizes Bible verses. That's so geeky. Is it weird that I find it tasty?"

"I was thinking the same thing, dude" responded Kim, watching her go.

Just then, Adoram flew in and landed right where Sharise had been sitting across the table from the guys.

"Greetings! The eyes of the Lord run to and fro throughout the whole earth, to show Himself strong on behalf of those whose heart is loyal to Him," the angel said to Rodney.

"Greetings, Adoram," replied Rodney, forgetting himself for a moment at the sight of the beautiful, huge, blindingly bright angel.

"Who is he talking to?" Elias asked Kim. Kim had a tough decision to make. He could share Rodney's secret vision with Elias, or tell Elias that Rodney was losing his mind. If he went the latter route, the school counselor would get involved, parents would be called, things would get messy. Fortunately for Rodney, Kim chose to go with the truth. Kim almost always chose to tell the truth. Except when a female asked him how she looked.

"Remember when he was in the hospital?" asked Kim.

"Yeah, you showed me that video. It was funny."

"It was hilarious. Anyway, it was around that time that he started to be able to see angels among us."

"What? Are you kidding me?"

"No, I am not."

"Wow," said Elias with a look of awe on his face. "Does he see Jesus, too?"

Rodney had sort of registered their conversation, and now he turned his attention to them for a moment. He felt a bit relieved that Elias now knew his secret and he wouldn't have to work so hard to hide it. "No, not Jesus," Rodney said. "Jesus doesn't have time to hang around me all day."

"Actually," Adoram corrected him, "Jesus exists outside of time. He has an infinite amount of time. He can spend all day with every created being for the entirety of their existence."

At that comment, Rodney turned his attention back to the angel while Elias looked on, fascinated that Rodney was having a conversation with someone or something not visible to everyone else.

"Really?" Rodney asked.

"Truly," said Adoram. "He wants you to know that."

"Wow. That's comforting because I'm gonna get beat up after school if I show up for that fight—which I probably won't. All because of a chick. I mean, I'm totally in love with Selefina, but I think I'm going to have to give her up in order to avoid getting pounded."

"He talks cray cray, but he's starting to make some sense," Elias said to Kim.

"Yeah. Thank God," Kim said to Elias. To the empty spot that Rodney was looking at, he added, "And you guys. Thank you, guys for protecting him and stuff."

"So why can't I see Jesus right now?" Rodney asked Adoram.

"*Geisterseherkraft* doesn't work that way. People just see angels and demons—who are actually fallen angels. They don't see God, Jesus, or even the Holy Spirit. Your limited minds can't process the face of God."

"Oh, I get it. So, what are angels, really?" asked Rodney.

"We are created beings, similar to you, but with more glory," answered Adoram.

"You aren't people who died and went to heaven?"

"No, definitely not. We were never human."

"Huh. How come the Renaissance painters make you look like fat, flying babies?"

"That is annoying. It has to do with Satan wanting us to seem less powerful than we really are and therefore be taken less seriously."

"Ooh, Satan's pretty sneaky, isn't he?"

"He is. But you don't have to be fooled by him. You know the truth. The God of truth has redeemed you. The entirety of His word is truth. Just continue to walk in that truth."

"I'll try," said Rodney. "Thanks. I feel a little better now." He looked down at his tray of food and finally realized how hungry he was. He reached for his fork, his stomach growling. The fork clattered to the floor and came to rest underneath the table. As Rodney bent over and closed his fingers around the wayward piece of cutlery, Kim said, "Watch your—" Bang! The table reverberated with the impact. "—head," he finished. Barook looked pained. He should have seen that one coming. Oops.

∭

By 4:35 p.m. the parking lot was crowded with kids anxiously awaiting a brawl. The Santa Anas were sending not only dry wind and dirt through the cars, but also a feeling of irritation (caused by negative ions) through the people gathered there. Sharise had asked her girlfriends to show up to support Rodney and to provide first-aid care. Elias and his friends were there, already praying for Rodney's safety. Half the soccer teamed turned out. Selefina was there, burning with excitement and lust. Rick was pacing like a caged animal, full of adrenaline and anger and jealousy. Selefina watched him with interest.

Rodney and Kim were working their way toward the center of the crowd. "I can't believe you talked me into showing up," Rodney whined.

"Well, you couldn't just run away. You aren't a coward."

"Have you met me?"

"Well, what would you have done tomorrow? Rick is in your physics class. You can't avoid him forever."

"I was willing to try."

"There you are!" Rick yelled at Rodney. "You're late!"

"I'm really sorry about that," Rodney began. Kim stayed close to his side in case Rick decided to make a lunge at his friend without warning. Adoram whispered in Rodney's ear, "Do not be afraid nor dismayed because of this great multitude, for the battle is not yours, but God's."

"You are definitely a sorry weirdo, that's for sure," retorted Rick. "I'm going to teach you a lesson about respect."

Adoram whispered, "Do not fear the reproach of men, nor be afraid of their insults, for the moth will eat them up like a garment, and the worm will eat them like wool. The Lord's righteousness, however, will be forever. His salvation is from generation to generation."

"Lord, save me now," Rodney said quietly.

Barook wandered over to Rick and stood by his right side saying calmly, "He's just a pathetic kid. He didn't do anything wrong. What are you really angry at?"

Just then Satan stepped out from the crowd and stood on the other side of Rick, talking into his left ear. "He's trying to take your girl away. Who does he think he is? He thinks he's better than you. He's mocking you."

"No, I'm not!" Rodney blurted out, answering Satan whom no one else could hear. Rick assumed Rodney was answering the insult he had thrown at him a few seconds ago.

"You are!" was all Rick could come up with in return. He wasn't a deep thinker. "And you'll be sorry!" Rick lunged forward so he would be in striking distance of Rodney's face. Rodney darted behind a car for cover. As Rick circled the car to get close enough to land a punch on Rodney, Rodney kept backing away, ducking behind other cars in an attempt to keep distance and a bunch of metal between him and his would-be assailant.

The crowd followed the action as it wove through the parking lot. Some kids ran ahead, trying to anticipate which way Rodney would go. None of them interfered, however, or got in the way of the fight.

"Keep in mind what is really bothering him," Adoram told Rodney as he hovered just above him. "This isn't about you."

"This isn't really about me, is it?" Rodney shouted toward Rick.

"What do you mean? Of course, it is. Now stop running away so you can catch these hands."

"I don't wanna bang 30s! I mean, how come you are wasting time throwing shade at me when there's a beautiful girl over there who is so thirsty for you?" Rodney pointed in Selefina's direction.

Rick swiveled his body around to look at her. She cocked her head and threw him her most flirtatious smile. Barook whispered in Rick's ear, "She likes you!" Satan countered with, "No, she doesn't! How could a girl like that not find you repulsive?"

Kim ran up to Rodney's side and whispered, "I think this is working. Keep going."

Rodney continued, "Selefina, you have a crush on Rick, right?"

"Maybe," she said, looking at Rick while she traced a circle with her dainty foot on the blacktop, not even bothering to make eye contact with Rodney.

"See, it's true," Barook said to Rick.

"Really?" Rick asked her.

"Well, you're just so macho, Rick."

"Me?"

"Yeah, you. And handsome."

A few kids in the crowd made some hooting and howling noises.

"And you think Rodney's a total dork, right?" Kim asked Selefina, hoping to get Rodney off the hook altogether.

"Ouch," Rodney said to his best friend.

"Yeah," Selefina answered, never breaking eye contact with Rick.

Her answer hurt Rodney more than a punch from Rick would have.

"Oh," Rick said, taking a few steps toward the girl of his dreams.

"Kiss her!" Sharise shouted from behind Elias. "Yeah, kiss her!" Elias repeated. The crowd quickly took up the chant. "Kiss her! Kiss her! Kiss her!"

Rick turned bright red. Selefina saw the hesitation and embarrassment in his face. She couldn't risk him losing his nerve and running away, so she grabbed him by his shirt, pulled him in close, and planted a long, romantic kiss on her new beau.

"Oh, gross," said Satan.

Rodney let out a huge sigh and sat down on the pavement right where he was, unable to hold himself up any longer. "Thank you, Jesus. And Adoram. And Barook." Kim and Elias slapped Rodney on the back and congratulated him on staying alive. Sharise and her friends Lynette, Viera, and Brie celebrated as well. But some others in the audience were disappointed that the fight was not going to take place after all. And Rodney was disappointed that he had lost the love of his life. Worse yet, it was possible that she never really liked him at all. His heart hurt.

Rick grabbed Selefina's hand and dragged her away from the crowd. "Let's go somewhere more private." He hated being the center of attention. And he wanted this moment with Selefina to last.

The rest of the kids, seeing that the spectacle was over, wandered off to their cars or to the waiting buses to go home.

"How's it going?" Adoram asked Satan.

"I think it's going well," Satan said in Jude Law's British accent.

"Do you now?" asked Adoram.

"Yes. He may have avoided bloodshed today, but that boy will snap like a twig when he sees what I have planned for him tomorrow."

"Hmmm," said Adoram, uncomfortable at the thought of what Satan might do next.

"Time to go!" The lord of the darkness flew off to tend to evil plans he had laid elsewhere.

"So soon?" asked Adoram as Satan disappeared. It wasn't like Satan to not use all of his allotted time to tempt Rodney. Adoram was not looking forward to tomorrow.

Kim lifted Rodney up off the blacktop. "You ready to go home, bro?"

"Yeah, I guess so. Elias, you want a lift home?"

"Sure, thanks man."

Rodney unlocked his Pacer and the boys climbed in. As Rodney maneuvered his silly car out of the parking lot with the angels hovering over its roof, he said, "I'm not sure how much more of this I can take. Jude Law is supposed to tempt me for three more days. As you can see, it's ugly."

"That's pretty real, dude," said Elias. "But you were great back there."

Kim added, "And that handsome demon is gone now, so you made it through today."

"No, I wasn't great back there," Rodney answered Elias. "I was terrified. I almost lost it. I thought I was going to pee my pants when I saw Rick. I'm glad you guys were there. I'm just so bad at this stuff. I don't have any life hacks for this situation. Kim, I wish this was happening to you. You would be so much better at this than me."

"That's true," said his best friend. "But that's only because I take my spirituality a lot more seriously than you do. I read the manual, dude. Every day. It's important to be prepared. God left us a road map. I want to study it. Just like I want to exercise my body and feed it good food; or to stimulate my brain and make it solve problems. It's important to me to be strong in my faith."

"It's because you're a total Type A personality," Elias teased.

"Yeah, that helps. And having a tiger mom goes a long way, too," Kim laughed. "But seriously Rodney, you have to get yourself together. This is not your ninth-grade science project. I can't save your butt. I don't know what the demons have planned for you, but it can't be good. And I doubt it's going to get easier. I gave you all those Bible study books last year. Have you read any of them yet?"

"No," Rodney admitted. "See? I'm such a loser!"

"Well, at least you still have time to do something about that. You're not an old man, you know. Even though you look like one."

"I guess," Rodney sighed. He didn't seem very motivated by Kim's attempt at a pep talk. Kim was worried about him. Rodney needed to get his mind right before the demons came back.

"Remember, God has not given us a spirit of fear, but of power and of love and of a sound mind," Kim said. "I'll pray for you tonight."

"Me, too," said Elias.

Chapter 10

Consider him who endured such hostility from sinners against himself, lest you become weary and discouraged in your souls. You have not yet resisted to bloodshed, striving against sin.

~ Hebrews 12:3-4

Saturday morning, Rodney woke up and texted Kim right away: "Hey corn dog."

Kim sent back, "Hey funnel cakes."

"U wanna hang out? I'm not looking forward to today."

"Come n get me."

Rodney quickly showered, dressed, and ran downstairs.

"Hey, Mom," he said upon entering the kitchen.

"Hey sleepy head," she responded. "You're moving quickly," she noted as he grabbed a granola bar out of the cupboard and headed toward the front door. "Where are you off to?"

"Kim's place."

"Okay. Back for dinner?"

"Probably."

"Well that's nice and precise. I'll probably have food for you, then," she said sarcastically.

Rodney didn't notice the tone in his mom's voice. His mind was on other things. "Thanks, Mom. Love you," he said as he skipped out the front door.

Rodney jumped in his Pacer. A few minutes later he pulled into Kim's driveway. Still in the car, he texted, "Im her." At the best of times, Rodney's sloppy texts were hard to read. At the worst of times, they were incomprehensible.

Kim emerged from his home, yelling behind him, "and stay out of my room! I mean it!" He slammed the front door and got into the Pacer.

"Sue being a snoop again?" Rodney asked.

"Yeah. What else is new? I need to go by the church for a minute, if you don't mind. I need to help them test a new camera for the live video stream tomorrow."

"No prob," said Rodney, backing into the street.

♪♪♪♪

Satan was in his study, sitting at a desk made of granite that seemed to rise from the stone floor like a wave. Shelves for books were carved into the stone walls on all sides. Books detailing every religion sat on the shelves alongside tomes on psychology, sociology, economics, and politics. Satan was talking on a secure land line when Tricklane appeared in his doorway. Satan waved him in as he continued his conversation. "Yes, Bob. That's right. And would you check our bitcoin balance? We probably need to buy some more. Get at least five million dollars' worth. Okay, make it ten. Call me tomorrow with an update." He hung up and asked, "What is it Tricklane?"

"Good morning, Dred Pirate Roberts. Your mention of bitcoin put me in mind of the dark web and The Silk Road that you built. That was so masterful."

"Yes, I know. Now there are many pirates and many illegal exchanges on the dark web. People can buy drugs and weapons, hire hit men, and sell counterfeit goods—all anonymously. It's wonderful, like Casablanca in the 1920's or Miami in the 1980's. But that's not what you came in here to talk to me about, is it?"

"I came to ask what you are planning to tempt Rodney with today."

"Oh, I'm not going to bother with Rodney today. I have reservations at the ICEHOTEL in Jukkasjarvi tonight. I want to get there early to see the reindeer."

"Ah, the place in Swedish Lapland! Well, I do know how you love to cool off once in a while. Would you like me to tempt Rodney in your stead?"

"What, you think yourself as good a tempter as me?"

"No, of course not, most devious one. I just thought that since you couldn't make it, I could step in as a poor substitute."

"No, let him expect me all day and worry himself sick. I've told you before that getting humans to worry over what might happen is often more effective than making something bad happen."

"Yes, your disgustingness, you have. That is an excellent plan, as always. Enjoy your time away tonight."

"I will. I always do. You can keep an eye on Rodney for me if you like. Let me know where he will be tomorrow if you can find it out without revealing yourself to him."

"I shall! Thank you for the assignment."

♫♫♫

Rodney pulled his car into the parking lot of The Church on the Way in Van Nuys. As he and Kim exited the car and entered the building, Kim said, "I'm going to find Jason. I'll only be a few minutes."

"I'll hang out in the sanctuary," replied Rodney. As he sat down in one of the pews facing the pulpit, Rodney noticed there were quite a few people milling about. He knew the sanctuary was large—it held about 800 people at one time. And he knew there were three services each Sunday which were always packed full. But he never figured some of the church's three thousand or so members would want to be at church on a Saturday. It had never occurred to him. Rodney noticed a person around his age sitting off to the far-right side of the room, about halfway down the rows of pews. Jumping all around the young man was a demon goat.

"Goat, goat. Where have I seen that before? Oh yeah, a lot of guys at school have goats around them." He wondered if certain shapes of demons denoted different things. "What does that mean, Bazooka?"

"A goat signifies lust."

"Oh. That's not good. I should go help that guy. He needs to get rid of that demon." Rodney started making his way toward the teenager.

"Be mindful of how frightening this can be for people. And be gentle. You will be revealing sins that are carefully hidden."

"Oh, I hadn't thought of that."

"I'm aware."

Rodney was wondering how to open the conversation with his target when he noticed the boy was watching something on his phone. Rodney chose to enter the row above where the young man was sitting. The seats in the church were long, upholstered benches. Rodney awkwardly shuffled sideways down the pew, then suddenly went down, tripped by a stray hymn book lost on the floor. Before Rodney landed on the carpet, Barook extended his wings around him. In Rodney's attempt to get back up, his arm knocked against the young man's feet in the pew below.

"What the?" the guy looked up and saw nothing. He twisted around in his seat in time to see a mop of red, curly hair emerge from behind the bench he was sitting on.

"Oh, hey there!" said Rodney.

"Um, hi. You good?"

"Me? I'm great. How about you? How are you doing?"

"Fine."

"Can I pray for you?"

"No thanks. I'm just waiting for my mom."

Rodney didn't expect this dead end. He still wasn't adept at reading other people's emotions or engaging with strangers. "Oh, no prob," he said. Rodney exited the pew and stood four or five rows behind the teenager who went back to looking at his phone, the demon goat still frolicking around him.

"What should I do, Bazooka? Can I pray for him from here?"

"Of course, you can."

Rodney began praying. As he did so, his eyes grew large as he watched lightning shot out of Barook's hands toward the goat. It bleated loudly for 20 seconds and then trotted quickly out of the sanctuary. "Wow! We did it!" Rodney exclaimed. "That was epic! Wait. What if it comes back?"

"It most certainly will. Or another one will take its place. It's not that easy to shake a pornography addiction. That's why you should be teaching people how to cast these demons out for themselves. It will empower them for the rest of their lives."

"Oh boy. I guess I still have a lot to learn." Rodney looked down at his feet. Then he looked up and around the sanctuary again. He saw a middle-aged lady praying in the third row from the pulpit. Her long, dark hair was tucked behind her ears. Her head was bowed. Her hands were folded together. A large buzzard sat on her back just below her neck. It pecked at the back of her head with its massive beak. Next to her sat her dominion angel who looked like an elderly woman with short white hair.

Rodney remembered seeing a buzzard on the back of his physics teacher at school. He whispered to Barook, "What kind of demon is the buzzard?"

"The buzzard is a spirit of depression. It is very hard to resist."

Rodney felt a deep urge to help the woman. He moved toward the front of the sanctuary. When he got to the row where she was seated, he said, "Excuse me, ma'am. I see that you are praying. Do you mind if I pray with you?" This wasn't an unusual request in The Church on the Way. It was a house of prayer. In every service, Pastor Temple built in time for the congregants to pray for each other. The woman acquiesced. "Yes, that would be nice. I'm having a hard time at my job right now. My boss lady is not very nice."

"And that makes you sad?" he asked gently while sliding into the pew next to her. "Scooch over."

"Oh, I don't have a right to feel sad," she said, sliding over so he could sit down. "So many of my friends and family have bigger problems than me."

"Well, sometimes sadness can sneak up on us for no reason. You shouldn't beat yourself up about it. But we should pray against that evil spirit."

"Oh, really? You think so?"

The woman's guardian angel shouted "Yes!"

"I'm pretty darn sure," said Rodney, almost laughing.

"Okay, mister. Go ahead." She took hold of Rodney's hands and closed her eyes.

"Dear Lord," Rodney paused and looked at Barook who told him, "Use the power of Jesus' name to cast it out and send it back to hell forever."

"Oh wait, what's your name?" Rodney asked the woman.

"My name is Maria."

"By the power of Jesus' name," Rodney continued hesitantly while fixing his eyes on the huge supernatural bird, "I throw you off of Maria and I send you back to hell forever." At that moment, the demon buzzard squawked loudly and flapped his wings. Maria's guardian angel shot lightning out of her hands at the buzzard.

The buzzard was thrown backwards ten feet. It flapped its wings furiously and flew out of the sanctuary.

"It's working!" Rodney shouted.

"It is?" asked Maria. "Who are you talking to?"

"I was talking to the demon on you. We did good! It's gone!"

"Oh, my! You are talking to demons? You are scaring me."

"Well, it was just the one. It's gone now. I'm sorry. I didn't mean to scare you. I guess I should dial it back a little. But I wanted you to be free of that evil spirit. If it comes back, or another one comes—"

"How should I know that?"

"Well, hmmm. I guess if you feel sad again, just pray against it."

"What do you mean?"

"Like I did. Just use the power of Jesus' name and His authority to get it away from you, to throw it out. You know what? I bet your boss has a spirit of anger clinging to her. And like you, she doesn't even know about it. Maybe you should pray against that when you see her next."

"You want me to talk to an evil spirit?"

"Well, you don't have to talk to it. Just pray against it. It might help."

"Does she have to know I'm doing that for it to work?" asked Maria with trepidation on her face.

Rodney looked at Barook who shook his head and said, "No, but make sure she prays out loud. It will be more effective. The demon will be able to hear her, and any surrounding angels will be able to hear and join in the fight, too."

"No," Rodney repeated to Maria. "Just make sure you pray out loud. But the boss lady doesn't have to know about it."

"Okay, mister. I do feel better now. Thank you for what you did. What did you say your name was?"

"I'm Rodney. It's a pleasure to meet you, Maria."

"You, too," she said, standing up. "Now let me out." As she exited the pew and started walking toward the door, she said,

"Maybe I'll see you Sunday." Her guardian angel waved goodbye to Barook and flashed the thumbs-up sign.

"I think that went well," Rodney said to Barook.

"You're getting better at this," Barook conceded.

Rodney scanned the sanctuary again. "What about that guy over there with the monkey on his back? What do monkeys mean?"

"Monkeys are spirits of anger. Be cautious."

Rodney began making his way toward a middle-aged man in a blue suit pacing at the back of the sanctuary. A demon capuchin monkey was screeching in his ear. The monkey had seen the commotion with the goat and the buzzard. It wasn't happy about being approached by a prayer warrior who knew how to get rid of evil spirits. The business man's guardian angel had also seen Rodney cast out those demons. He was excited to see Rodney coming their way. He had been trying to tell his human about the demon on his back, but to no avail. The man just felt like his anger was from inside and kept condemning himself for it instead of seeking freedom from it.

Because of Barook's warning, Rodney thought he should try a different approach with this person. "Excuse me, sir. Would you mind praying for me?"

"What? Why? What do you need?" he asked, somewhat irritated. He hadn't noticed Rodney praying with the others moments ago.

"I'm having issues with feeling like a loser. You seem like a successful person. I thought maybe you could help me get my confidence back."

The businessman softened at the compliment and the request for help. "Oh, sure, son. Come on over here." The man laid his hand on Rodney's shoulder, bowed his head, closed his eyes, and began praying, "Lord, grant this young man the grace to know how much You love him and value him. Bless him with the understanding that God is able to make all grace abound toward him, that he may have sufficiency in all things, and an abundance for every good work."

"Amen!" said Rodney. Then, with his own head still bowed and eyes still closed, he took the chance to pray, "Lord, thank you for this gracious man and his powerful prayer. In the name of Jesus, I speak against the spirit of anger plaguing him and I throw it off of him forever." Rodney looked up slightly and saw the demon monkey being pushed off the man's back by the lightning coming from the hands of his guardian angel.

The man in the suit looked up at Rodney, "How did you know?"

"Um, it was the Holy Spirit, I guess," said Rodney.

"I feel like such a weight has been lifted. It never occurred to me to pray against that. I can't thank you enough."

"Gosh, you're welcome, sir."

Just then Pastor Jack Temple approached the two. "Sorry I kept you waiting, John. Come on back to my office. Rodney, that was some impressive praying. Maybe you'll join us for the Wednesday night prayer service? I think you could help a lot of people."

"Oh, wow," said Rodney. "Yes, sir. I'd like that."

As Pastor Jack and John walked out of the sanctuary, Kim walked back in. "K, dude. I'm ready. Let's go to Corky's and get something to eat."

♪♪♪♪

A few blocks away, Selefina was chatting on the phone with her handsome new boyfriend. "I got into a fight with my stepdad this morning. He's always telling me what to do. He has no right to boss me around and make me clean the house. I hate him. I want my father back."

"Really?" Rick asked. "What's he like?"

"I think he's nice. I don't know. I was so young when he got deported. You know, I thought that was the government's fault. But then I heard my mom talking to her friend, Cecilia. She actually said, 'If you want to stay in this country legally, just tell them that Juan hit you.' Can you believe she said that?"

Rick was confused. "Why would she say that? That doesn't make any sense."

"Because Cecilia's daughter is a citizen."

"I still don't understand."

"Let me tell you the rest of the conversation. You'll see. Cecilia said, 'But Juan doesn't hit me. He loses his temper sometimes. And sometimes he breaks things when he's mad drunk. But he doesn't hit me.' And then my mom said, 'Well, just wait until he breaks something one night, call the police, and tell them that he hit you in the stomach. He can't prove he didn't. Then he will get arrested and deported and you will get your U-Visa. You will be able to stay here and work as long as you want. How do you think I did it?' She actually said that! She actually said that she lied about my dad and got him deported! It's so disgusting! I'm so mad at her!"

"Oh, babe, I'm sorry. That's terrible. What can I do to help?"

"Just take me somewhere lit tomorrow. I don't wanna think about it anymore."

"What about Clifton's downtown?"

"The cafeteria? I heard about the fancy remodel. That sounds good. Is it expensive?" She was hoping it was expensive. She had heard that it was just as amazing, if not more so, than the 1935 original with a brand new, giant tree in the center of the restaurant reaching three stories high, and the original taxidermized bear, bison, and lioness in dioramas throughout.

"No, don't worry," said Rick. "It's not expensive."

Selefina hid her disappointment.

∫∫∫∫

Rodney and Kim were sitting in a booth at a diner originally built in 1958. The place was currently called Corky's. It was built in the Googie style by architects Armet and Davis as Stanley Burke's Coffee Shop. Located on Van Nuys Boulevard in Sherman Oaks, it still claimed loyal customers of all ages even though ownership had changed more than once throughout the decades.

The food at Corky's was fresh, the prices were reasonable, and the service was friendly. Rodney felt like celebrating, so he was really glad Kim wanted to come here. The 60's vibe made him feel good and the portions were big enough to satisfy a teenage appetite. Rodney was sawing his way through a crispy piece of chicken-fried steak smothered in white gravy while retelling his prayer successes in the church to Kim. Barook and Koram were sitting in the booth too, alternately watching the boys, scanning the room, and chatting with each other. "You should have seen it. Lightning was shooting everywhere; demons were flying all over the place. It was a madhouse! You would have loved it!"

"Sounds epic, dude."

"It was. The pastor asked me to come back on Wednesday night for the prayer service and help pray for more people."

"Whoa. That's quite an honor. I've never been asked to do that," said Kim with a twinge of jealousy.

"I'm not sure I'm up to it, though. What if I can't do it? What if it was just today? I might screw it up on Wednesday night."

"If God gives you the will to serve Him in a certain way, He's also going to help you do it. He won't ask you to give what you don't have. Don't worry so much."

"Yeah, I guess you're right. I just get so nervous sometimes." At that moment the demon Tricklane was crouched down outside the wall of the restaurant, underneath the window where the boys were eating. From here, Rodney and the angels couldn't see him, but he could eavesdrop on the two friends' conversation.

"I know, dude."

"And I'm nervous about this whole temptation thing. My demon buddy hasn't shown up yet today. What is he waiting for? Does he have another event he wants to take me to tonight? Will he bring more cupcakes? Will someone else want to fight me? Is he gonna try to get me to use meth? After today, I still have two more days of temptation to live though. I'm not sure I can handle it all."

"Well, we can hang out all day today. And tomorrow we can go to church in the morning. I have a feeling your demon won't want to show up and pester you there. Maybe that's why you haven't seen him today. And you said praise music bothers him. So be sure to keep that playing. We can go to the high school Bible study right after church. That will get you through to about 11 a.m."

"Sounds good. I like it. I really don't want to be alone."

"K. Let me see if I can find something for us to do in the afternoon." Kim pulled out his phone and activated the browser. "I'll check *LA Weekly's* event calendar." After a few seconds of scrolling he said, "Oh, dude, this is perfect! There's a soul food and gospel music festival happening in downtown L.A. tomorrow. BBQ, fried catfish, and music from church choirs. Check this out: Chance the Rapper is going to headline! We have to do this. It starts at 11 a.m."

"That's perfect."

"Uh oh."

"What's wrong?"

"Tickets are $50 each. I've been saving money from my job, but how are you going to afford it?"

"Oh. I think I'm going to have to tell my parents."

"Everything?"

"The whole megillah. Seeing angels. Demons tempting me. There's no way they are going to shell out $50 for me without hearing the whole saga. Even after they hear the whole saga, they might not want to give me the money. We'll see, I guess."

"Do you want me to help you tell them?"

"Would you? It's going to be awkward."

"Don't I know it. But that's what friends are for— uncomfortable conversations with your family." Kim shuddered at the thought.

"I can't thank you enough," said Rodney.

"Well, one day I will call on you for a really uncomfortable favor, and you will have to deliver."

"That seems fair." Rodney stuck out his hand and they shook on it. As they did so, Rodney's elbow became firmly planted in his mashed potatoes and gravy. "Oh, man. Not again," he moaned. Outside the restaurant, Tricklane backed away from the window and made his way down the street to a law firm. In a closet there, he crossed into the dimension we call hell.

♪♪♪

It was getting late on Saturday night. Rodney was in his bedroom listening to praise music and chatting with Barook. Kim had gone home after dinner. Their conversation with his parents went extremely well. They had way too many questions about angels, heaven, demons and hell that he couldn't answer, but Kim's presence had helped a great deal. Kim even managed to convince them that Rodney wasn't schizophrenic. They had agreed to buy a ticket for him to the soul food and music festival. And when he asked if they would spring for a ticket for Elias, too, well they thought it was sweet and they went for it. He hadn't seen that coming.

But still, Rodney was uncomfortable. He asked Barook, "Isn't Jude Law going to visit me today? He's running out of time! What is he up to? It's freaking me out."

Barook responded with, "Well, he has the right to tempt you every day until Tuesday morning. He can only come once per day. But he doesn't have to come every day. I suppose he can skip a day if he thinks that might be more effective. Fear of the unknown is quite powerful."

"Yeah! It's terrifying not knowing what's going to happen. Or when. I hate this."

"Relax, child. The wicked flee when no one is pursuing them, but the righteous are as bold as lions. Remember, God has not given you a spirit of fear, but of power and of love and of a sound mind."

"Of power and of love and of a sound mind," Rodney repeated to himself. He changed into his pajamas and climbed into bed while meditating on what Barook had said. He hoped sleep would wash over him quickly. It had been a momentous day and he was wiped out. He was looking forward to spending Sunday with Kim and his crew. He was sure everything would be alright tomorrow. But he was young and he still had a lot to learn about Satan.

Chapter 11

Behold, I have made you this day a fortified city, and an iron pillar, and bronze walls against the whole land. They will fight against you but they shall not prevail, for I am with you, says the Lord, to deliver you.

~ Jeremiah 1:18-19

It was Sunday morning in hell. Satan, in full military regalia, moved around the front of a large, dark cave with stone walls. Demons of all shapes and sizes were standing in formation before him. The dragons, being the largest, were in the back. Angry monkeys were screeching in the front, occasionally smacking each other. Hyenas were behind the monkeys, nipping at the monkeys' heels and howling. Rats were scurrying everywhere and frogs were clinging to the walls, croaking loudly. Roaches, locusts, cicadas, and other flying bugs were flittering about the disgusting crowd.

"Enough! Shut up!" screamed Beelzebub. "This mission is important to me! Tricklane, are they aware of their duties?"

Tricklane, who was standing in the shadows at the front of the room answered, "Yes, sir! To swoop in and terrorize Rodney and all those around him at the time and location of your choosing this afternoon!" he shouted. "They will be on standby here, awaiting your order. I will be with you. Once you have made the decision, I will come here and lead them to the right spot. They know that gospel music will be playing and that people will be praising God loudly. They are prepared to face that awful situation. They will be strong! They will not fail!" The demon monkeys starting making excited little screams and the hyenas whined slightly with anticipation.

"And do they know the stakes?" the Accuser bellowed.

"Yes, sir! Success in this mission will be rewarded with an upgrade in rank!" he yelled back. "Failure brings demotion and three days of torture!"

"Fine, fine. I must leave now," Satan said more calmly. "Come, Tricklane, let's finalize the plans in my office. And get rid of that drooling monkey. He disgusts me."

"Slagbag? Yes, sir! He does drool overly much, sir. Consider him gone!"

Satan and Tricklane flew through the cave system quickly back to Satan's office. The monitors on the wall there were displaying examples of the work that Satan's underlings were executing. On a few of the topmost monitors, fake news was being displayed across Twitter and Facebook. On the bottom left monitor, a demon snake was telling a gang banger, "Why not start a church? You could get away with anything if people think you're a man of the cloth. That white collar will get you into any door. Young girls will trust you. It will be easy."

A monitor near the middle of the wall displayed the horror fiction website Creepypasta Wiki. It showed the legend of The Slender Man along with stories and doctored photos uploaded by horror fans who wanted the creepy myth to seem more real. The black-suited Slender Man, when anyone caught a glimpse of him throughout the centuries, was always tall—maybe eight or ten feet—and skinny. Sometimes he had tentacles coming out of his back. He was rumored to kill children, or maybe he just took them to another dimension. Either way, the children were never seen again according to the legend and the fan fiction around it.

A monitor next to the Creepypasta Wiki showed two 12-year-old girls, Anissa and Morgan, in shackles in a Wisconsin courtroom. They had taken The Slender Man legend to heart and tried to kill their other girlfriend, Payton, as a sacrifice to him, to impress him. Morgan was suffering from schizophrenia and psychotic spectrum disorder at the time. Payton, despite being stabbed 19 times, was able to crawl to a pathway next to the woods where she was attacked. A man riding a bike down that path at just the right moment saved her life by calling an ambulance.

Although Anissa and Morgan would later be found not guilty of attempted second-degree homicide by reason of insanity, they would be sentenced to spend 25-40 years in mental health institutions. Multiple families would be devastated by this one incident. It was a ringing demonic success.

Satan looked at the monitors. "The misinformation campaigns are going well. People will believe anything they see on the internet. It's almost too easy these days. I think some of my crew are going soft."

"Well, we can toughen them up with a little torture," Tricklane answered.

"What did you have in mind?"

"A six-month tour traveling with the group Up with People."

"Oh Tricklane, that's so cruel. I love it. And how are the UFO sightings coming?"

"Pretty well. Your flights to heaven and back in your spaceship always bear fruit. Plus, we can easily manipulate light for nighttime sightings. We've managed to get *The X-Files* back on the air. Most people in the world believe in at least the possibility of extraterrestrial life. The Pope supports the possibility. The Vatican Observatory is ready to welcome extraterrestrials as brothers. Organizations like SETI are looking for proof of intelligent alien life. It won't be hard to manufacture that proof when the time is right. I think we are well poised for an 'encounter' whenever you are ready for that type of manifestation."

"I might need to save that big reveal until such time as the appearance of the anti-Christ. I think it will give him instant credibility and his powers will be more believable if he is assumed to be from outer space."

"Excellent plan, sir."

"In the meantime, keep the sightings up at a consistent pace."

"Will do, sir."

"I have to head back to heaven now for another meeting. I'll fill you in when I return."

"Yes, sir. Safe flight, sir. Hurry back. I know how you hate it there." Tricklane saluted his master.

♫♫♫♫

Satan was traveling along a golden street in heaven chatting with Adoram. The usual angelic guard detail was surrounding them. "Why does everything have to be so bright here?" Satan asked petulantly.

"Well," Adoram began.

"That was rhetorical. I know the answer: light, truth, blah, blah, blah. You're all so happy and fulfilled, I just want to barf."

"It's great to spend time with you, as well, old friend," responded Adoram.

"Can we just get this over with?"

"Who's stopping you from getting to the point? Tell me what your plans are for Rodney and you can be on your way, lickety split."

"What?" Satan stopped abruptly. The angels behind him wielding flaming swords almost ran into him. "I don't have to go to Gabriel's office?"

"No. You can give your report to me today."

"Great, then. Here it is: I won't bother him during church in the morning."

"So kind of you. Too many angels there to deal with?" Adoram smiled.

"But in the afternoon," Satan continued, ignoring the interruption, "probably while he's at his music festival, I will launch a full assault with one legion of demons. That should be enough to turn him into a puddle of a human being. It should only take a few minutes."

"Thank you for the information and for playing by the rules. You may go now."

"Yay," said Satan sarcastically. He did a 180 and made haste back to the dock where his spaceship was waiting. Adoram watched him go, guarded all the way by warrior angels. He then turned around and continued on his path to Gabriel's office to update the archangel.

♫♫♫

Rodney woke up Sunday morning feeling somewhat satisfied but still apprehensive. He thought about the good he had done yesterday at church. He was proud of himself for finally serving

God and advancing His kingdom. He felt good about telling his parents the truth about his *geisterseherkraft*. And it was terrific fun when he invited Elias to the soul food and music festival. He would text Sharise this morning to see if she was going, too. She loved gospel music; he figured she probably had purchased tickets weeks ago.

As he was getting dressed for church, finishing the lumpy knot of his tie, Adoram flew through his bedroom window. "He makes His angels spirits, and His servants a flame of fire!" he trumpeted upon landing. Rodney was so startled, he nearly choked himself with his tie. "Oh! Hi there! You scared me."

"I come not to frighten but to edify," Adoram said.

"I'm glad to hear it because I'm really nervous about what today will bring. I'll be honest; I'm not sure I can handle any more tempting. This is all just too much, I think," he said as he sat down hard on the bed. The bed expressed its dissatisfaction by creaking. "Is there any way we can just call all of this off?"

"Why are you so fearful? How is it that you have no faith? After all that you have seen and done, should you doubt the power of the Lord? I tell you, the Lord will go before you, and the God of Israel will be your rear guard!"

"Yeah, I hear that," Rodney said, trying to buck himself up. He started picking up socks from the floor and sniffing them, looking for the least offensive pair to put on. "Maybe I can even believe it if I try really hard."

"Let's get you downstairs to breakfast and then to church. Jude Law won't bother you there," promised Adoram. "Plus, your dad's making bacon. You love bacon. Even when he burns it."

"That sounds good," agreed Rodney. The smell of bacon almost overcooking downstairs helped motivate him to put on his socks and shoes quickly.

"Let's just take this day one hour at a time," said Adoram.

"Good plan," said Rodney.

♫♫♫

Sitting in the pew at church, his parents on one side of him and Kim on the other, Rodney felt safe. Pastor Temple was preaching on the life of Job. Rodney could relate.

"Now here's what I find so interesting," the pastor said. "A lot of people quote Job 1:21 where Job says, after losing all of his children and his livestock, 'Naked I came from my mother's womb, and naked I will depart. The Lord gave and the Lord has taken away; may the name of the Lord be praised.' While I find it commendable that Job continued to praise God, even in his tragedy, Job got it wrong. The Lord did not take away. It was the devil who did the taking. The Lord, in the end, restored everything the devil took and then some. In chapter 42, verse 12 it says, 'The Lord blessed the latter part of Job's life more than the former part.' So let's not make the mistake of thinking that God likes to punish us by cursing us. In all of Jesus' time on earth, He never cursed or punished anyone. He never made anyone sick to teach them a lesson or help them be a better person. He never refused to heal anyone who asked for it. Our God is a good and generous God. James says, 'Every good gift and every perfect gift is from above, and comes down from the Father of lights, with whom there is no variation or shadow of turning.' That's the Father we have. That's the takeaway from Job's experience."

The sermon made Rodney feel a little better, but he still wouldn't let Kim leave his side during Bible study. When that was over, they went to pick up Elias.

♫♫♫

Rodney's Pacer pulled into a parking spot at the North Hollywood metro station. Three teenage boys spilled out of the small car. As they walked toward the entrance of the subway station Kim asked, "Why are we taking the subway?"

"It's the parking, dude. It will be like $20 or something crazy to park downtown. Don't worry, we're meeting Sharise and her friends here. It will be fun. We can all ride in together."

"I hate the subway. The sights, the sounds, the smells— urine, vomit, stale beer, body odor. It's just so basic," complained Kim.

"Nah, it's gritty," argued Rodney. "Besides, YOLO."

"No Rodney, Kim's right," Elias said. "It's disgusting. I sat in coffee last week. At least, I hope it was coffee. Plus, there's never any security when you need it. Thanks so much, by the way, for this ticket. It was really chill of your parents."

"Yeah, they can be woke sometimes," Rodney answered. "I just have to wash all the dishes, do all the laundry, and clean the bathrooms for the next month."

Kim laughed. "I have to do that all the time. And I don't get paid for it."

Rodney mimed playing a violin. "That's because your mom is mean."

"Yeah, sorta," replied Kim with a smile.

They entered the station and walked downstairs to buy tickets for the red line train to downtown.

"There's Sharise," said Kim, pointing to the train platform.

The boys touched their tap cards to the turn-styles, walked through, and joined her on the platform.

"Hey guys! Here's my squad," she said by way of introduction, pointing out the ladies one by one, "Lynette, Viera, and Brie."

"Howdy," said Kim, wincing directly afterward.

"Where did that come from?" Rodney asked. "Why on earth did you say that?"

"Oh, we have a cowboy among us," teased Lynette, shaking his hand. She tossed her long black dreadlocks behind her shoulder with one hand and laughed. Kim was simultaneously embarrassed and impressed with her snark. "What's your name, partner?" she asked with a gleam in her eye.

"Kim."

"You. Are. Kidding. Me. You know that's a girl's name, right? Isn't that embarrassing for you?"

"It's not half as embarrassing as my first name," Kim replied.

"Oh, what's that?"

"Soo-Hee."

"Um, you're right. Kim it is," declared Lynette.

Kim had heard it all. Those who didn't think he was a girl compared him to North Korea's young Supreme Leader, Kim Jong-Un. He had often thought about changing his name, like his sister had done. Ultimately, he had decided he would rather be interesting than comfortable.

"Um, hi" said Elias cautiously. "My name is Elias. That's a boy's name."

"You have nice skin," said Brie sweetly. Elias was thinking the same thing about her. "Brown is beautiful, right?" he replied.

"Hey ladies," said Rodney trying to be slick but coming off as oily.

"Oh, Lord, save us from this one," said Viera rolling her green eyes.

"Here's the train. Thank you, Jesus," Sharise said, mortified by that round of introductions. The girls would never let her live this down—hanging out with such uncool guys, even for an afternoon. She rushed through the subway train's doors as soon as they opened, barely letting the exiting passengers out first. She found a cluster of seven open seats together and quickly sat down to claim them.

The seats on L.A.'s subway trains are unlike any other subway seats anywhere in the world. Maybe the planners were trying to be forward-thinking. The plastic seats are covered with cheap fabric that feels like astro-turf. Perhaps this fabric is easier to clean—a simple hose down at the end of each night might be all that's needed. But it's also problematic. The fabric is multi-hued with garish purples, blues, and yellows. It resembles unicorn puke. It makes it impossible for commuters to tell whether a seat has recently been soaked with coffee or urine or water, or anything for that matter. Many seasoned commuters simply put their hands on the seats before they sit down to feel for unpleasant surprises.

As the group settled in around Sharise, Rodney noticed Selefina and Rick enter the train and sit down a few rows in front of them. "Oof!" he exclaimed, his stomach tightening at the thought of confronting Rick again. The fact that Selefina was so enamored with Rick made him feel sick, too.

Kim followed his gaze. "Oh, it's Selefina and her new bae. They look happy."

Selefina and Rick sat down near the train doors in a row that faced a perpendicular seat reserved for the disabled or elderly. Selefina used that reserved seat as a footstool.

Sharise looked over at her. "Ugh, that girl is so self-centered! Not only is she keeping people from sitting there who need to, she's getting the seat dirty. So not chill."

"That ain't it!" said Viera in protest to Selefina's action.

Just then an LAPD officer contracted by the Metro Transit Authority boarded the train and began walking down the aisle looking at the passengers. He was there to make sure there were no unauthorized animals, no loud boom boxes, no bicycles in any car but the front or back, no one eating or drinking, no one groping anyone else, no one smoking, no one passed out, no one selling socks or candy, and no fights breaking out. The subway in Los Angeles wasn't for the faint of heart.

"Hey, look," said Elias. "Some security. How weird is that?"

"Young lady," the police officer said as he reached Selefina, "put your feet down."

As Selefina looked up at the officer, her demon snake hissed in her ear, "How dare he? Who does he think he is?" Selefina haughtily uttered "Excuse me?" as she raised her eyebrows.

"Oh, no she didn't!" said Lynette with surprise on her face. "Who is that girl?"

"Take your filthy feet off the seat in front of you," said the officer, already losing his patience. "We're trying to have a society here."

Selefina's snake spat, "He thinks he's your father. Everyone wants to tell you what to do!" She said flatly, "You can't tell me what to do." She was sick of adults bossing her around and messing up her life.

"I can, actually. You're breaking the rules and I'm an officer of the law."

"Hey, bae," pleaded Rick next to her, "just take your feet down. It's rude."

"This is not going to end well," said Sharise as the group watched in fascination and horror. "That man does not know who he's dealing with."

"I wish I had some popcorn right now," said Viera clapping her hands in delight.

"If you don't take your feet down right now—,"

"What are you going to do about it?" challenged Selefina.

At that, the officer grabbed her by the arm and began dragging her off the train as he called for backup via his shoulder walkie-talkie.

"Get your hands off of me!" Selefina screamed, wriggling and resisting, grabbing onto a pole to keep from being pulled out the train doors. "I paid to be on this train!"

Rick jumped up and stayed next to her without actually interfering with the officer. He was dumbstruck. He didn't know how to defuse Selefina. No one did. But he respected the law and knew she was in the wrong. He liked her a lot, but he wasn't willing to go to jail for her.

"Oh, this is too good!" said Brie who pulled her phone out and started recording the incident.

"Out you go, little missy," the officer said with a final wrench, successfully getting her out of the train and onto the platform as two more uniformed police officers ran down the stairs to assist.

Lynette stood up and began clapping. Viera jumped up and followed suit. "Thank you, officer, for removing that pest!" she shouted. Soon the whole train was applauding the officer. He just nodded and proceeded to handcuff a raging Selefina. The train's doors closed and it began moving away from the station.

"Well, that was fire!" said Kim. "You don't see that every day."

"You don't ride the subway every day," said Elias with a laugh. "The red line is no joke. You know the most amazing thing about that encounter? The fact that someone was patrolling the train." The group laughed and chatted about what they had seen for the next five stops, but an uncomfortable feeling nagged at Rodney. It was really hitting home to him how influential the spirit world could be.

♫♫♫

As the friends entered Grand Park, set between The Music Center and City Hall in downtown Los Angeles, Adoram flew down and landed next to Rodney.

"I don't want to frighten you, but you need to be prepared for what is coming. A legion of demons will attack here this afternoon. I have called in angels to fight for you, but you need to give them all the assistance you can. Do you understand?"

The blood drained from Rodney's face as he listened to Adoram's speech. He nodded slowly as he walked with his friends who were surveying the landscape.

"Remember how you prayed against the demons in church? Use that technique again. Be a conquering warrior. You can do this. The Holy Spirit will also help you in your weakness. When you do not know what you should pray, the Spirit Himself will make intercession for you with groanings which cannot be uttered."

Rodney was still absorbing the impact of what Adoram was telling him when Kim announced, "I'm hungry. I'm going to get some smacks from that BBQ booth right there."

"What are you doing?" Rodney screamed. "You can't just hit the first food booth you see! That's cray cray! You need to check them all out, compare notes, and then make an informed decision. This is reckless! What if you see something better on the other side of the park?"

"I'm hungry now," said Kim, pulling out his wallet.

"Bad call, cowboy," said Lynette. "I'm with the redhead. He's not wrong. You can always circle back to this booth once you know you haven't seen anything better."

"See?" Rodney exclaimed, stretching out his hands to emphasize the point. Kim was having none of it. That perfectly cooked meat in front of him smelled delicious. The line was short.

It was only $5 for a small plate of ribs. He just ignored everyone and got in line.

"We have a man down," Rodney said. "But we can recalibrate. We can make it through this."

Elias was worried at how worked up Rodney was. He seemed so anxious for no good reason. "It will be fine, Rodney. Let's give him a few minutes to grab his food and then we can begin the recon of the rest of the food booths. It's all good, buddy. Just calm down. You're Draking."

"You're right. You're right. I know you're right. It's just that . . . well, I need to tell you guys something. You're going to think I'm insane, but I need your help. So just bear with me. Even if you don't believe me, I need you to pretend that you do. Can you all do that?"

Elias and the girls nodded, filled with curiosity. Rodney continued, "At some point today, some demons will visit me and even launch an attack on me—maybe on all of us, I don't know for sure. When the time comes, I need you all to pray. Pray hard. Pray out loud that by Jesus' authority these demons will be thrown into the lake of fire forever, never to return. Can you all do that?"

"Um, yeah," said Sharise. "Are you sure you want to be in public with all this going on?" She was a little worried that he was having a mental breakdown. She thought breakdowns were better had in private.

"This was Kim's idea. I think it's a good one. Pretty soon the gospel music will start. Demons hate that. The praise songs will help repel them. Plus, it will make me feel better."

Elias saw the worried looks on the faces of the girls and decided to help. He recounted to them how Rodney had gained the power to see demons as well as angels after having the trampoline accident at church. Sapphire, Sharise's guardian angel, whispered in Sharise's ear, "He's not crazy. Just trust him and do what he asks. What could be the harm in praying?"

Sharise turned to her friends and said, "What could be the harm in praying on cue? I'm in."

"I'm in, too," said Lynette.

"K, then," said Viera. "This is weird, but fine."

"I'll help you, Rodney," said Brie. "You seem like a nice guy. A little odd, but nice."

Kim rejoined the group just then, munching on a beautiful, moist, tender pork rib slathered in a tomato-vinegar-brown sugar sauce. Lynette said to him, "You know you're going to have to give me one of those, right?"

He smiled and moved the cardboard container toward her. She pulled a rib from the pile and took a bite. "Mmmm, that's good. You might have made the right decision, after all, partner," she conceded. "So, just to catch you up on what you missed, we're going to start praying against demons when your friend here tells us to." She pointed the rib bone at Rodney. "Apparently there will be some kind of attack here this afternoon."

Kim raised his eyebrows. He hadn't expected Rodney to let the whole group in on his secret. And this was the first he heard of an attack. "But how are we going to fight the demons if we can't see them, Rodney? You're the only one who will know what they're doing."

"You don't have to be able to see them in order to conquer them. You don't want to see them. Trust me on this one. All you need to do is pray when I give you the signal."

"Oh no," said Viera. "I'm not keeping my eyes fixed on you all afternoon waiting for a signal. Just start shouting."

"K," said Rodney. That was probably a good idea, he figured. He would most likely start screaming when he saw the demons attack anyway and forget whatever signal he had set up. This girl was pretty smart.

"Great plan," said Lynette. "Now let's go check out that booth selling po' boys. I think they have a fried shrimp and oyster combo."

"Oh, that sounds good," said Kim.

Lynette was shocked. "You just ate! You are still eating right now!"

"But you haven't eaten yet, and you owe me a bite," he said with a sly smile.

Elias patted Rodney on the shoulder, "See? Everything is going to be fine."

Rodney looked at Elias and said, "Yeah, what could go wrong?"

♬♬♬

Chance the Rapper was performing his song "Angels" on the low stage set up in downtown L.A.'s Grand Park. The Soul Food & Music Festival was packed with people enjoying themselves on a beautiful Sunday afternoon. "I got angels all around me, they keep me surrounded," sang Chance. Rodney looked around at all the angels surrounding him and his Christian friends as they stood in a clump amongst the crowd enjoying the music. He noticed the angels' glory was reflecting off of the clouds in the sky, giving golden edges to the puffy white clumps of atmosphere.

Suddenly, Rodney caught sight of some motion from the west. Dark-winged dragons were flying toward him at a high rate of speed. Thousands of demon roaches and cicadas quickly filled the air around him and above him. Rodney felt choked with terror. Giant spirit apes loped in from all sides and began bellowing and screeching in the crowd near him and his friends. Satanic hyenas began biting at the concert goers, putting them on edge and making them feel irritated. All Rodney could do was tug on Kim's sleeve. He couldn't speak; his eyes were wide with horror. When Kim looked over, Rodney weakly pointed to the sky and began whimpering. Then he dropped to the ground, curled up in a ball, and began rocking himself gently.

"It's go time, people," Kim shouted. Elias nodded and began praying aloud, "Lord Jesus, protect us all from these demons. I claim your authority and I speak against these dark forces. I command that they return to hell and stay there forever!"

Sharise began praying in tongues. Her girlfriends were shouting, "Amen!" and "Thank you, Lord Jesus!" and "I agree with him, Lord Jesus. Let it be done as he has said, Father God." As they prayed, the guardian angels were empowered to shoot lightning from their hands at the legion of demons attacking the crowd. Some people began pushing and shoving each other, getting into shouting matches with very little provocation.

Adoram unsheathed his flaming sword, flew into the sky, and began slicing through the dragons who were shooting their quills of pain into the people below. Rodney, still curled into a ball, rolled onto someone's foot accidentally. "Get off me, weirdo!" the man shouted. He gave Rodney a kick to drive his point home. Kim threw himself between Rodney and the violent man saying, "Hey, dude. He needs mercy right now, if you don't mind."

The guardian angels were deflecting the blows of the gorillas and the biting hyenas, making progress driving them away as the rest of Rodney's friends kept praying. Barook took on two gorillas at once, shooting a lightning ball out of each hand. They hit the gorillas in the chest, knocking them back a step or two and singeing their fur.

Koram landed a spinning back kick on a hyena, throwing him three feet away from Kim. He then took aim at another hyena advancing on his charge. His front kick sent the demon five feet into the air. Koram flapped his wings furiously to clear the space around him of the flying demonic insects.

Elnathan stood back to back with Sapphire, their white wings spread wide. They slowly ascended and surveyed the scene. Demons were everywhere, but the angels outnumbered them. Lightning flew from Elnathan's hands at every demon he could spot. First one to the left of him, then another straight ahead. Sapphire was lobbing lightning balls into the fray. They acted as heat-seeking missiles, finding their marks on the nearest demonic heads.

The man who kicked Rodney was no longer surrounded by demons. Instead, angels were all around him. He immediately felt regret for his outburst. "I'm sorry. I don't know what came over me," he said to Kim. "I hope your friend is okay." He walked away quickly, ashamed of his actions. Rodney could feel the darkness around him begin to subside. He opened his eyes to see a legion of angels slaying the demons and driving them all back to hell. He could hear his pal Jude Law scream, "Those are some of my best fighters!" at Adoram. "How dare you?"

Adoram retorted, "This was your idea, remember?" as he powered his flaming sword through three more demon gorillas. The rest began running away.

Rodney uncurled himself and stood up with Kim's help. "It's working. It's really working," he said pathetically. He saw Elias and the girls praying, and a strong light coming down from heaven toward them. The light broke into prisms as it hit the prayer warriors, shining forth all around them. He saw the angels driving the demon force back and many demons retreating on their own. "I can't believe it! We're winning!" he shouted at Kim.

"That's great news, bruh."

Soon, there were no more demons left in the sky or on the ground. Only Satan was left facing Adoram and a thousand angels. "Fine. You win. This time," he said. Then he flew off to the nearest portal to hell which happened to be located in the back office of a car dealership a mile away.

Rodney was panting with emotional exhaustion. He tapped Elias on the shoulder and said, "We won. You did it. It's over."

"Praise God!" Elias shouted.

"All glory to Him!" Sharise said.

"Amen!" said Lynette. "I could actually feel power going out of me. That was unbelievable."

"You guys were incredible," said Rodney, wiping tears from his face. "I was pathetic. But you guys—you did it. You did it all and you saved me. You weren't afraid at all."

"We couldn't see what you could," Kim reminded him.

"But I failed," said Rodney.

"Hey, there is no condemnation in Christ," said Elias gently, patting Rodney on the shoulder.

"Yeah, we all fail sometimes," said Sharise, giving him a one-armed hug.

Adoram came close to Rodney, "You are the righteousness of God in Christ."

"I don't feel righteous."

"It's not a matter of feeling, it's a matter of acceptance. What makes you think you can undo God's righteousness by sinning? It was a gift to you. Just like you can't undo your sinful nature by doing good works, you can't ruin your righteousness by sinning. Jesus paid your ransom. He redeemed you."

"But how? How can that be?"

Kim noticed that Rodney wasn't talking to the group anymore. "Here he goes," he said to them, holding up his index finger. "Let's give him a minute." The group went back to watching the concert and congratulating each other.

Adoram continued, "Because Jesus, who knew no sin, took your sin upon Himself at the cross so that He could give you His righteousness."

"That seems like a bad deal for Jesus."

"Well, His thoughts are not your thoughts, nor are your ways His ways. As the heavens are higher than the earth, so are His ways higher than your ways, and His thoughts than your thoughts."

"Yeah, I guess that's true," said Rodney, slowly accepting the lesson that Adoram and Barook had been trying to teach him for days now.

Suddenly, Rodney seemed to snap out of his trance. He looked around at his friends, filled with gratitude and love. "I'm starving," he announced to everyone. "Let's go around those food booths one more time."

"I saw some peach pie over there." Kim pointed across the lawn.

"Let's go get it. I'm buying!" Rodney said triumphantly. "Because I am greatly blessed and highly favored!"

"Amen!" shouted Lynette. "And it was cobbler, fool, not pie" she said to Kim. "Cobbler."

Chapter 12

For this purpose, the son of God was manifested: that he might destroy the works of the devil.

~ 1 John 3:8

Rodney got home from the soul food and music festival around 10 p.m. He was exhausted, physically, emotionally, and spiritually. He couldn't help but feel victorious, even though he knew it was his friends who deserved most of the credit for helping the angels to win the battle over the demons. He wasn't sure what Monday would bring, but he knew he should get as much sleep as he could in order to face whatever trial Jude Law had cooked up for him. He brushed his teeth quickly and climbed into bed in his undershirt and boxers. "Goodnight Bazooka. Thank you for all you did for me today. And thank you for always being by my side."

"Goodnight, Rodney. It is my honor to be by your side. And I will be here when you wake."

Rodney's waking was much sooner than he expected. Around 2:30 Monday morning, Satan flew through his window and landed on his bed with a thud. Rodney sprang awake. His eyes beheld the most terrifying sight: a dark cherub who towered at least ten feet over him. The creature shone as though he were made of polished bronze. He was glowing, but it was not from glory. It was the dark energy of outrage, envy, and hate. He had four wings that spread out behind him. His head contained four faces. The one pointed at Rodney was the face of a man. On the right side of Satan's head, Rodney could see the face of a lion in profile. To the left side, the face of an ox was outlined in the dark. Rodney couldn't see the face of an eagle on the back of Satan's cherubic head. But he could see that this creature also had eyes all over his body, blinking, seeing eyes. Where his feet should have been were whirring wheels, set within wheels, something like two giant gyroscopes.

"Come with me," said the creature. His voice sounded like a roaring crowd of people. It hurt Rodney's ears. He was overcome with fear and dread. He couldn't move or speak. Barook laid his hand gently on Rodney's head and said, "Fear not. God is with you. He will strengthen you. He will uphold you with His righteous right hand. Satan can't harm you. He will, however, try to get you to harm yourself. With him, it's always a mental challenge. Don't give in to his false ideas and wrong thinking."

The lord of evil had arms like a man located just underneath his slowly flapping wings. He reached down with his right arm and took Rodney's hand. Instantly they were transported to the top of Mt. Kilauea.

It was half past midnight in Hawaii. The mountain was dark; no Hawaiian Volcanoes National Park rangers were around. The guard in the Thomas A. Jaggar Museum was reading a book. There were usually no tourists visiting this late at night. Even if he had looked out of the window next to him, he wouldn't have noticed a small guy sitting down in the dark by himself. Rodney was hidden by the wooden viewing platform that was open to the public. He and Satan had appeared on the caldera of this shield volcano in the space where tourists weren't allowed to roam because it was so unsafe there. Kilauea had been active for the past 3,000 years, sometimes violently. It had been slowly oozing lava through two rift zones further down the island since 1983. Recently, those rifts spewed lava dramatically, destroying houses and reforming the landscape into barren, black rock.

Rodney, from where he was sitting on the ground, could see the red glow of the hot lava contained in the caldera below them, bubbling underneath its cooled, black, floating crust. He could feel the heat of it on his face. It gave Satan's cherubic form an ominous red outline. He wondered if this were the lake of fire that Satan would be thrown into one day. "Lord, if I were a real man, I'd throw this demon down there now," he prayed to God. "Who am I kidding? I'm no hero, Father." Satan rolled around the edge of the crater a few feet to Rodney's right. It seemed to Rodney that he was riding a Segway. Satan leaned forward and his wheels within wheels propelled him ahead. He leaned left and he rolled left. The eyes all over his body were blinking, but not quite in unison. It was very distracting. It was all Rodney could focus on. Some eyes were blinking quickly, others were blinking very slowly and languidly. As Satan rolled back toward Rodney, one eye on Satan's leg was watering a bit. Maybe the dirt being kicked up by the wheels was irritating it, Rodney thought. Or maybe it was the sulfur dioxide in the air from the volcano.

Rodney kept his attention on the blinking eyes because he couldn't let himself feel the fear in the pit of his stomach. He wanted to vomit. He had never known such dread in his life. This presence before him was so evil. It wasn't charming or handsome or even British anymore. It was simply terrifying. Rodney felt as frail as a hummingbird in a hurricane before this horrific creature.

"Who do you think you are?" Satan bellowed at Rodney. "Are you so important that this should be happening to you?"

"No," said Rodney. "I'm no one. I'm nothing." As he said it, he felt the full weight of that statement sinking into his soul. He prayed to God again. "I'm so unimportant, Lord. No one in my family relies on me for anything. I don't exactly mentor foster children. I don't volunteer at the homeless shelter. The cat doesn't even care whether I exist or not. My Grammy and Grampy are dead. No girls at school think I'm cute, or even interesting, especially Selefina. If I die tonight, Lord, most people in my life would barely notice. I mean, my parents would care. But that's about it."

"You are a child of the most high God," corrected Barook. The voice startled Rodney. He hadn't even noticed that Barook had followed him on this horrible trip. He was glad to see his guardian, but the feeling of horror and deep depression remained. He just didn't believe what Barook had said.

"You're no saint," the Father of Lies spat. Do you think you are so pure you can withstand me?"

Rodney thought about this. He bowed his head and began confessing his sins to God. "Forgive me for all the terrible things I've said to my parents. Forgive me for cheating on that math test I didn't study for. Forgive me for procrastinating so long on my ninth-grade science project that Kim ended up doing all the work. Forgive me for failing to keep my fast when that demon who looked like Jude Law showed up with cupcakes. Was that demon the same as this guy, Lord? Was Jude Law Satan in disguise all along? Because I thought he was just some random low-ranking demon. I'm so stupid. I thought this temptation thing would be more fun." To Satan, he said, "I'm not pure at all. I'm chock full of sins."

Barook didn't like how dejected Rodney looked and sounded. He knew that Satan could act as a spirit of depression, however. And that he could be very hard to resist, especially on so little sleep. He whispered to Rodney, "God made Jesus, who knew no sin, to be sin for you, that you might become the righteousness of God in Him."

Rodney bowed his head again and prayed, "I don't deserve Your protection or righteousness or forgiveness, Father."

"That's right. You're pathetic," said the King of the Darkness.

"I know," agreed Rodney. "I'm a loser. I have no purpose in life. No one will ever love me. I'm ugly. I'll never have a family. I'm not good at anything. I'll never do anything great like cure cancer. I'm so pathetic." He turned his eyes skyward, beheld a heaven displaying the full glory of the milky way and shouted, "I have no idea why You created me, God!"

"You're a waste of space," crowed the demon. "Not that it matters. Life is pointless anyway. You think high school is miserable? It gets worse. You'll get a job you hate. You'll be disrespected, disregarded and despised constantly. Life is one long, hard slog."

"I know. You're right. My own dad told me that I won't amount to anything and that life will be one long feeling of frustration." Tears were streaming down Rodney's face. He wrapped his arms around his chest and whispered to God, "I feel so hopeless and unloved. Help me. What is the point of this life?" Barook's heart was breaking watching this scene unfold.

"You should just throw yourself into this volcano and get it over with," suggested Satan softly. "Put yourself out of this misery. What's the point in going on?"

"You're probably right," agreed Rodney. He couldn't imagine that he would ever contribute anything to society. He would probably never have kids. He wasn't exactly advancing the kingdom of God, he thought. He had never saved even one soul. He felt so worthless.

"I can see how much you're hurting," said the angel of light gently. "Just jump and the pain will be gone. It will all be over. No more agony. Just jump and find peace."

Rodney looked over the edge into the abyss and contemplated his own destruction.

Barook was horrified. Not surprised, but horrified nonetheless. Satan was hard to resist. It was time for some tough love. "How dare you even consider hurting yourself when Jesus hanged on the cross for you?" he demanded of Rodney. "This is a form of self-righteousness. You think you can pay for your own sins or make up for what you lack by killing yourself? Well you can't. It's the ultimate act of selfishness. You think it all ends when your body dies?"

"No, no I guess not," Rodney sniffled.

Satan immediately changed his tack, latching onto Barook's last thought. "But heaven will be wonderful. You'll get to be with God, singing His praises all the day long. Don't you want to go there now? Just jump and you'll be there in a flash. You won't feel a thing, I promise. I'm doing you a favor. Look how easy and painless I've made this for you. Most people can't escape this terrible life with so little effort. All you have to do is stand up and fall over."

Barook knew the temptation that Christians sometimes felt to go home and be with their savior sooner than He had planned. "Wait, Rodney," he said. "Christians can't just kill themselves because heaven is a better place than earth."

"Why not?" demanded Rodney in frustration.

"Do the math. Let's play this scenario out to its natural conclusion. No one is left on earth to save the lost. No Christians are left to point the unsaved to the way, the truth, and the light. Who will teach them to live life with a due sense of responsibility, not as those who do not know the meaning of life but as those who do? You are here for a reason. If you extend your soul to the hungry and satisfy the afflicted, then your light shall dawn in the darkness, and your darkness shall be as the noon day. The Lord will guide you continually, and satisfy your soul in drought, and strengthen your bones. You shall be like a watered garden, and like a spring of water which does not fail."

"Oh," said Rodney, beginning to understand.

Satan began roaring like a lion, terrifying Rodney to his very soul. Barook continued, raising his voice above the din, "For the Son of Man did not come to be served, but to serve, and to give His life a ransom for many. He thought it worthwhile to come here to save souls. Even your soul. You can't stay here and spread His love just a little while longer?"

"I don't understand His love. I don't get why Jesus loves me so much." Rodney's eyes were pleading with Barook. He wanted to understand so badly.

"You're not a father yet," Barook said gently. "Maybe when you are, that will help you understand."

"You'll never be a father!" shouted Satan with his booming voice. "You'll never be anything."

"I happen to know the plans that God has for you, Rodney," said Barook. "Plans for peace and not evil. Plans to give you a future and a hope."

"Really?" Rodney asked weakly.

"Really," said Barook.

"Are not two sparrows sold for a copper coin? And not one of them falls to the ground apart from Your Father's will. But the very hairs of your head are all numbered. Do not fear therefore; you are worth more than many sparrows."

"I am?" asked Rodney.

"Yes!" Barook shouted. "You are!"

"He's lying!" roared Satan.

"No, he's not!" Rodney shot back. Satan's attack on Barook's credibility made it clear to Rodney that he shouldn't listen to anything Satan said. "I am worth more than many sparrows," Rodney said more boldly. He might not believe that he was a hero, but Rodney's fragile ego could hold onto the idea that God thought he was worth at least a bundle of birds.

Satan roared some more. Rodney was terrified, but he kept repeating his new mantra over and over. "I am worth more than many sparrows." It seemed to shut Satan up for a little while.

At that moment, back in L.A., Kim woke from a fitful sleep. Koram was leaning over his bed, slapping him in the face. "Good, you're awake. Rodney needs help. Send me to him!" Kim took a moment to gather his thoughts. "Lord, please help Rodney right now," he prayed aloud. He wasn't sure why, but he felt compelled to do so. "Send your angels to protect him." With that, Koram flew out the window and across the ocean to Hawaii.

He landed on the crater's edge next to Rodney and told him, "I'm here to help. Kim sent me. He's praying for you."

"Wow," said Rodney. "That's so nice. I can't believe it." At that moment, Elnathan flew in. "Elias sent me to help you, Rodney. Remember, in all these things—tribulation, distress, persecution, peril—we are more than conquerors through Him who loves us."

Rodney thought about this for a moment. And about his friends who loved him enough to pray for him in the middle of the night. Suddenly Sapphire appeared. "Let me guess. Sharise is praying for me?" Rodney asked her. The lady angel nodded and smiled.

This gave him the courage he needed to shake off the oppressive spirit of depression that had a grip on his soul. He grabbed a fistful of dirt and threw it in some of the eyes covering Satan. The blinking stopped. The eyes hit by the dirt stayed closed. Rodney picked up more dirt next to where he was sitting and threw it in more of Satan's blinking eyes. His hand closed around a rock. He picked it up and hurled it at his nemesis.

"Tell me what to do!" Barook shouted. "Give me permission!"

"In the name of Jesus, I command you to drive Satan away!" Rodney screamed. He looked at Barook to see if that had been the right prayer. Barook pointed his hands at Satan and balls of fire shot toward the evil one.

The guard inside the Hawaiian Volcano Observatory was looking out the window now. "Is that lightning? Hey, you! Kid! What are you doing out there?" The guard banged on the window. Rodney didn't respond to the noise at all. Officer Ho quickly made his way toward the building's exit so he could pull this stupid teenager off the crater's edge. He had pulled other suicidal kids off the edge before. No one was going to die on his watch. "Get away from the edge, kid! Don't do it! I know life seems tough right now, but it will get better," he shouted at Rodney.

"I'm not going to kill myself!" Rodney shouted at Satan. "I'm going to trust God to get me through this!" Lightning bolts, sizzling with God's fury, shot from Barook's hands at Satan. Koram and Elnathan joined in, sending volleys of fire and lightning Satan's way. Satan was thrown back ten feet.

"It's working!" yelled Barook.

"Good, good" said the guard moving slowly towards Rodney. "Now come away from the edge."

After a few more volleys of lightning and fire balls from the angels, Satan departed with an enormous, deafening scream. Rodney was stunned. Barook was ecstatic. For the first time,

Rodney noticed the guard coming towards him. "How are we gonna get home, Bazooka?"

"Call Adoram."

"I don't have his cell number."

"No, call out to him. Use your voice."

"Adoram," Rodney called out quietly.

"A little louder," said Barook.

"He can hear me even if he's not here?"

"Yes. And God conveys your prayers to us. So, give him a shout."

"Adoram!" yelled Rodney.

"No, my name is Alika," said the guard. "Now come on over here, please. I don't want you to fall in accidentally."

Over the guard's shoulder, Rodney could see a pinpoint of light in the distance. It seemed to grow larger and larger every second. A moment later, flapping his six white wings and glowing with glory, Adoram appeared before them.

"I wanna go home," Rodney said to the seraph angel, bursting into tears.

Adoram grabbed Rodney's hand and a second later they disappeared.

"Whoa! Where did you go, buddy?" asked the very confused guard. He would spend the next 30 minutes getting too close to the crater's edge himself looking for a red-headed teenager who wasn't there anymore.

Back in Rodney's bedroom, Adoram, Rodney, and Barook materialized. The other three angels had gone back to their duties. Adoram spoke first. "Blessed is the man who endures temptation, for when he has been approved, he will receive the crown of life which the Lord has promised to those who love Him."

"Thanks, Adoram. And thank you, Bazooka. And I need to thank Koram and Elnathan and Sapphire when I see them next. And thank you, Jesus, for loving me so much, even to the point of death. I don't get it, but I'm starting to accept it," Rodney said.

"You need to consent to be loved by God, to allow Him to shepherd you. Accept His grace. Remember, it's a gift; you can't earn it. You don't even need to try. Let Him wash your feet. Let Him heal your heart. Let Him love you." Adoram walked over to Rodney's window. A flaming sword appeared in his hand. "I will guard you for the rest of the night, son. Now get some rest."

"K," said Rodney, still in his undershirt and boxers. He climbed back under the covers and was snoring in under a minute. He dreamed he was a pelican, flying low over the ocean waves. Three pelicans were flying to his left, and four were keeping pace with him on his right side. One by one the other birds dove underwater. Rodney dove, too. Then he was somehow swimming underwater. He had never seen a pelican do this in real life, but his dreams were always a little sketchy. It was like the part of his brain assigned to write his dreams took shortcuts sometimes. He never questioned it while he was dreaming.

Along he swam, the other pelicans still beside him, a few feet below the surface of the waves. Then his pelican companions began bursting into the sky. Rodney followed them, but something was different. The other birds were flying free, but Rodney was encased in a bubble of water, even though he was now above the waves. He couldn't flap his wings, he couldn't breathe. He began to panic as he kicked his feet furiously and shook his head. Finally, the water trap around him burst, and Rodney was free. Water droplets exploded in all directions as he spread his wings wide, flapped them hard and climbed gracefully into the air to join the other birds, finally free.

ʃʃʃʃ

Rodney pulled up outside Kim's house Monday morning to take him to school. As Kim was jumping in the car, Rodney blurted out, "Satan came to see me last night."

"Satan himself? No wonder you look so bad."

"Yeah."

"Really? The big guy? The original snake in the garden?"

"Yeah. Except he didn't look like a snake. He looked freaky. Bazooka told me just now that Satan is a cherub angel. Did you know that?"

"I'm not sure I did. Weird. What did he look like?"

"He had six wings. And arms, like Adoram."

"Who's Adoram?"

"He's the supervising angel. I told you about him. Bazooka's boss. He's a seraph angel. Technically he outranks Satan. He is of a higher order. Neat, huh?"

"Um, yeah. Go back to what Satan looks like."

"Oh, right. He's huge. He has legs, but he looks like someone attached a Segway to his ankles instead of feet."

"He's a cyborg?"

"Maybe. He moves around on these spinning wheels. And get this—this is the grossest part—he has eyes all over his body. Eyes, dude. They blink and everything."

"Oh snap! Really?"

"Does he have eyes in his head where they should be?"

"Yeah. But he has extra faces. He has his man face. That's in front. Then, on one side he has an ox face. No joke. And on the other side he has a lion face. Then, in the back of his head where hair should be, he has an eagle face. It's so creepy. You should have seen it. It weirded me out so badly. It was worse than any movie monster I've ever seen."

"It was worse because it was real, bruh."

"Yeah, probably."

"So, what happened?"

"Well, it was the middle of the night. He touched my hand and poof! We were staring down at a volcano."

"What? A volcano? Where?"

"I have no idea. Maybe it was Colorado. I'm not sure. It was cold."

"I don't think Colorado has any—"

Rodney cut him off. "It doesn't matter where, exactly. The fact is, we were on the rim of a volcano and Satan tried to get me to jump into it—into the churning lava below. He wanted me to French-fry myself."

"Are you kidding me?"

"No, it was awful."

"How did you get out of there? What did you do?"

"Well, I knew you were praying for me," said Rodney with a grateful expression.

"How did you know that?" asked Kim, embarrassed.

"You sent Koram over to help me."

"Oh yeah, I did. That was a good idea, huh?"

"It was a great idea. And guess what? Elias sent his angel, too. And so did Sharise."

"No way!"

"Way."

"Wow, that's awesome."

"It was. It helped a lot. Then I threw lava rocks and dirt at Satan. And the angels shot him up with lightning. And he went away."

"Good job, dude. I don't know if I could have done that."

"Yeah, I wasn't a coward for once."

∫∫∫∫

Satan stood in Gabriel's office in heaven, waiting for the archangel to finish serving them tea.

"Ready to admit defeat?" Gabriel asked, handing Satan a cup of Darjeeling.

"Defeat? Are you crazy? I won! You saw him cowering in fear at the music festival on Sunday. He did nothing to stop me. That makes me the winner."

"No," Gabriel corrected him. "Being overcome with fear is not the same as losing your faith. Being an inactive Christian is not the same as losing your faith, either. What counts as a victory in hell is not always a failure in heaven. We deal in mercy here. And grace. And forgiveness. Besides, Rodney was smart enough and faithful enough to teach his friends how to overcome you and a legion of your best evildoers. And he resisted your ultimate temptation on Monday. You were right. I do have a strong saint now. He's stronger now than he ever would have been without your interference."

"You cheater! You liar! You're changing the rules after the game is over."

"You know that I'm not," Gabriel said with infinite patience for God's fallen creation.

"I hate you so much!" Satan screamed. "You are the worst!"

"I'm sorry you feel that way. Adoram, you may escort him back to his ship now."

"Why do you treat me like this?" Satan yelled over his shoulder at Gabriel as he was being ushered out of the room.

"Because with lies you have made the heart of the righteous sad; and you have strengthened the hand of the wicked, so that he does not turn from his wicked way to save his life," Gabriel responded sadly as he watched Satan go.

∫∫∫∫

The alarm on Rodney's phone began blaring at 6:30 a.m. Tuesday. Rodney didn't want to get up, but he only had 30 minutes to get showered, have breakfast, and leave for Kim's house so that they could be in class by 7:40 a.m. He rolled out from under his covers, stood up, and almost tripped over some dirty clothes. Barook righted him just in time. He wandered into the bathroom to start his shower. Adoram flew through the window just then.

He held up a new supervisory contract, similar to the one he and Barook signed on the ceiling a week ago. "I have assurance that this will work."

"It's only been a week since my last review. Will it be powerful enough?"

"We'll find out. Now come over here and we'll ratify it on the floor, just to make it easy."

"Right. Let me just put his sneakers here so he's more likely to trip over them."

The two angels got down on the floor and laid the contract between them. Simultaneously they pressed their thumbs against the holy paper. It began to glow with heaven's glory. Rodney burst out of the bathroom and took a look at the angels on the floor.

"Watcha doin'?"

"Come and see," said Barook.

Rodney, still toweling his hair dry, walked toward the angelic duo and tripped over his shoes. He fell face-first into the glowing contract. "Hey! Where did you guys go? I don't have time for hide-and-seek. I gotta get dressed." He pulled himself off the floor and began rummaging through T-shirts in his dresser. "We can do this after school."

Adoram, still on the floor with his thumb on the glowing contract said to Barook, "I think it worked."

"I think you're right. Rodney! Can you hear me?"

Rodney seemed oblivious to the angel's call as he continued to throw clothes on his body in a haphazard manner.

The angels stood up and watched Rodney bounce around the room. "He's going to miss seeing us," said Barook with a touch of sadness in his voice.

"Yes, but this is for the best."

"You're right, of course."

"Maybe he will retain a bit of his ability to sense your presence, to sense this realm, now that he's seen it for himself."

"I hope so."

"I mean, if certain messages got through to him," Adoram said while staring at a pen and notepad on Rodney's desk, "it wouldn't be so unusual because of his past experience."

"Oh, I see what you mean," said Barook brightening.

"I'll be going now. Take care of him. Shout if you need me."

"Thank you, sir, for everything."

"Keep up the good work, Barook." Adoram spread his six, beautiful, white, angelic wings and flew back to the HeavenLink downtown.

Rodney pulled on his shoes, grabbed his bookbag, and ran downstairs to the kitchen. He yanked a container of yogurt out of the fridge and ate it in 30 seconds flat. Then he pulled two frozen waffles out of the freezer and slid them into the toaster. As they were cooking, he poured himself a bowl of Cheerios and greedily tucked in.

Up in Rodney's room, Barook picked up the pen and wrote, in beautiful calligraphy, "I will always be near you, by your side, protecting you, for the rest of your life. There are more angels working for you than there are demons working against you."

Scripture Verses Referenced

Chapter 1

Genesis	28:12	He had a dream in which he saw a stairway resting on the earth, with its top reaching to heaven, and the angels of God were ascending and descending on it.
Isaiah	6:2-3	Above it stood seraphim; each one had six wings: with two he covered his face, with two he covered his feet, and with two he flew. And one cried to another and said, "Holy, holy, holy is the Lord of hosts; The whole earth is full of His glory!"
Ephesians	6:11-12	Put on the whole armor of God, that you may be able to stand against the wiles of the devil. For we do not wrestle against flesh and blood, but against Principalities, against Powers, against the Rulers of the darkness of this age, against spiritual hosts of wickedness in the heavenly places.
Ephesians	6:13-16	Therefore take up the whole armor of God, that you may be able to withstand in the evil day, and--having done all--to stand. Stand therefore having girded your waist with truth, having put on the breastplate of righteousness, and having shod your feet with the preparation of the gospel of peace; above all, taking the shield of faith with which you will be able to quench all the fiery darts of the wicked one.
Ephesians	6:17-19	And take the helmet of salvation and the sword of the Spirit--which is the word of God--praying always with all prayer and supplication in the Spirit, being watchful to this end.

Chapter 2

Chapter 3

Chapter 4

1 Peter	5:8	Be sober, be vigilant, because your adversary the devil walks about like a roaring lion, seeking whom he may devour. Resist him, steadfast in the faith, knowing that the same sufferings are experienced by your brotherhood in the world.
Luke	10:21	I thank you Father, Lord of heaven and earth, that You have hidden these things from the wise and prudent and revealed them to babes.
Luke	10:23-24	Blessed are the eyes which see the things you see, for I tell you that many prophets and kings have desired to see what you see, and have not seen it, and to hear what you hear, and have not heard it.
Psalms	25:4-5	Show me Your ways, O Lord; Teach me Your paths. Lead me in Your truth and teach me, For You are the God of my salvation; On You I wait all the day.
Psalms	32:8	I will instruct you and teach you in the way you should go; I will guide you with My eye.
II Timothy	3:17	Through the Word we are put together and shaped up for the tasks God has for us.
Psalms	119:130	The entrance of Your words gives light; It gives understanding to the simple.
Job	11:12	An empty-headed man will be wise when a wild donkey's colt is born a man.

Chapter 5

Matthew	26:41	Watch and pray lest you enter into temptation. The spirit indeed is willing, but the flesh is weak.

Ezekial	28:12-15	[about Satan and the King of Tyre] You were the seal of perfection, full of wisdom and perfect in beauty. You were in Eden, the garden of God; . . . You were the anointed cherub who covers; I established you; you were on the holy mountain of God; you walked back and forth in the midst of fiery stones. You were perfect in your ways from the day you were created, 'til iniquity was found in you.
Ezekial	28:16-17	By the abundance of your trading you became filled with violence within, and you sinned; therefore I cast you as a profane thing, out of the mountain of God; and I destroyed you, O covering cherub, from the midst of the fiery stones, your heart was proud because of your beauty; you corrupted your wisdom for the sake of your splendor; I cast you to the ground.
Daniel	10:5-6	I lifted my eyes and looked, and behold, a certain man [the archangel Gabriel] clothed in linen, whose waist was girded with gold of Uphaz! His body was like beryl, his face like the appearance of lightning, his eyes like torches of fire, his arms and feet like burnished bronze in color, and the sound of his words like the voice of a multitude.

Chapter 6

Daniel	11:32	but the people who know their God shall be strong and carry out great exploits.
Romans	6:14	For sin shall not have dominion over you, for you are not under law, but under grace.

Romans	5:20-21	Moreover, the law entered that the offense might abound. But where sin abounded, grace abounded much more, so that as sin reigned in death, even so grace might reign through righteousness to eternal life through Jesus Christ our Lord.
I Corinthians	10:13	No temptation has overtaken you except such as is common to man; but God is faithful, who will not allow you to be tempted beyond what you are able, but with the temptation will also make the way of escape, that you may be able to bear it.
Psalms	91:3-4	Surely He shall deliver you from the snare of the fowler and from the perilous pestilence. He shall cover you with His feathers and under His wings you shall take refuge.
Psalms	91:11-12	For He shall give His angels charge over you to keep you in all your ways. In their hands they shall bear you up lest you dash your foot against a stone.
Luke	10:10	Behold, I give you the authority to trample on serpents and scorpions, and over all the power of the enemy, and nothing shall by any means hurt you.
Psalms	91:13	You shall tread upon the lion and the cobra, the young lion and the serpent you shall trample underfoot.
Daniel	12:10	Many shall be purified, made white, and refined, but the wicked shall do wickedly; and none of the wicked shall understand, but the wise shall understand.
II Timothy	2:26	and that they may come to their senses and escape the snare of the Devil, having been taken captive by him to do his will.
Ephesians	5:25-26	Husbands, love your wives, just as Christ also loved the church and gave Himself for her, that He might sanctify and cleanse her with the washing of water by the word

1 Samuel	16:23	And so it was, whenever the spirit from God was upon Saul, that David would take a harp and play it with his hand. Then Saul would become refreshed and well, and the distressing spirit would depart from him.

Chapter 7

Job	34:21	For His eyes are on the ways of man and He sees all his steps.
I Corinthians	6:12	All things are lawful for me, but all things are not helpful. All things are lawful for me, but I will not be brought under the power of any.
I Corinthians	6:13	Now the body is not for sexual immorality but for the Lord
I Corinthians	6:18-20	Flee sexual immorality. Every sin that a man does is outside the body, but he who commits sexual immorality sins against his own body. Or do you not know that your body is the temple of the Holy Spirit who is in you, whom you have from God, and you are not your own? For you were bought at a price; therefore glorify God in your body and in your spirit, which are God's.
James	4:7	Resist the devil and he will flee from you.

Chapter 8

Ecclesiastes	7:8	The patient in spirit is better than the proud in spirit.
Jeremiah	17:7-8	Blessed is the man who trusts in the Lord and whose hope is the Lord. For he shall be like a tree planted by the waters which spreads out its roots by the river, and will not fear when the heat comes; but its leaf will be green, and will not be anxious in the year of drought nor will cease from yielding fruit.

Jeremiah	9:23-24	Let not the wise man glory in his wisdom, let not the mighty man glory in his might, nor let the rich man glory in his riches, but let him who glories, glory in this. That he understands and knows Me, that I am the Lord, exercising lovingkindness, judgement, and righteousness in the earth. For in these I delight says the Lord.
Romans	6:14	For sin shall not have dominion over you, for you are not under law, but under grace.

Chapter 9

Psalms	37:7-8	Rest in the Lord and wait patiently for Him; Do not fret because of him who prospers in his way. Because of the man who brings wicked schemes to pass. Cease from anger and forsake wrath; Do not fret--it only causes harm.
Isaiah	26:3-4	You will keep him in perfect peace Whose mind is stayed on You, because he trusts in You. Trust in the Lord forever, for in YAHWEH, the Lord, is everlasting strength.
Proverbs	3:5-6	Trust in the Lord with all your heart and lean not on your own understanding. In all your ways acknowledge Him and He shall direct your paths.
Zechariah	4:6b	"Not by might nor by power, but by My Spirit" says the Lord of hosts.
Romans	8:31-32	What then shall we say to these things? If God is for us, who can be against us? He who did not spare His own Son, but delivered Him up for us all, how shall He not with Him also freely give us all things?
II Chronicles	16:9a	For the eyes of the Lord run to and fro throughout the whole earth, to show Himself strong on behalf of those whose heart is loyal to Him.

Psalms	31:5	Into Your hand I commit my spirit; You have redeemed me, O Lord God of truth.
Psalms	119:160a	The entirety of Your word is truth
II Chronicles	20:15b	Do not be afraid nor dismayed because of this great multitude, for the battle is not yours, but God's.
Isaiah	51:7-8	Do not fear the reproach of men, nor be afraid of their insults, For the moth will eat them up like a garment, And the worm will eat them like wool; But my righteousness will be forever, And My salvation from generation to generation.

Chapter 10

Hebrews	12:3-4	For consider Him who endured such hostility from sinners against Himself, lest you become weary and discouraged in your souls. You have not yet resisted to bloodshed, striving against sin.
Acts	16:16-18	Now it happened as we went to prayer that a certain slave girl possessed with a spirit of divination met us, who brought her masters much profit by fortune-telling. This girl followed Paul and us and cried out saying, 'These men are the servants of the Most High God, who proclaim to us the way of salvation.' And this she did for many days. But Paul, greatly annoyed, turned and said to the spirit, 'I command you in the name of Jesus Christ to come out of her.' And he came out that very hour.
II Corinthians	9:7b-8	God is able to make all grace abound toward you, that you--always having all sufficiency in all things--may have an abundance for every good work.
Philippians	2:12-13	Continue to work out your salvation with fear and trembling, for it is God who works in you to will and to act according to His good purpose.

Philippians	1:6	being confident of this very thing, that He who has begun a good work in you will complete it until the day of Jesus Christ
Proverbs	28:1	The wicked flee when no one pursues, But the righteous are bold as a lion.
II Timothy	1:17	For God has not given us a spirit of fear, but of power and of love and of a sound mind.

Chapter 11

Jeremiah	1:18-19	For behold, I have made you this day a fortified city, and an iron pillar, and bronze walls against the whole land. They will fight against you but they shall not prevail, for I am with you, says the Lord, to deliver you.
Daniel	5:23	the God who holds your breath in His hand and owns all your ways, you have not glorified
Hebrews	1:7	Of the angels he says: He makes his angels spirits, and His servants a flame of fire.
Mark	4:40	But He said to them, "Why are you so fearful? How is it that you have no faith?"
Isaiah	52:12	For the Lord will go before you, And the God of Israel will be your rear guard.
Job	1:21	Naked I came from my mother's womb, and naked I will depart. The Lord gave and the Lord has taken away; may the name of the Lord be praised.
Job	42:12	The Lord blessed the latter part of Job's life more than the former part.
James	1:16-17	Do not be deceived, my beloved brethren. Every good gift and every perfect gift is from above, and comes down from the Father of lights, with whom there is no variation or shadow of turning.

Romans	8:26	Likewise the Spirit also helps in our weaknesses. For we do not know what we should pray for as we ought, but the Spirit Himself makes intercession for us with groanings which cannot be uttered.
Isaiah	55:8-9	For My thoughts are not your thoughts, nor are your ways My ways,' says the Lord. 'For as the heavens are higher than the earth, so are My ways higher than your ways, and My thoughts than your thoughts.'

Chapter 12

1 John	3:8b	For this purpose the Son of God was manifested: that He might destroy the works of the devil.
Ezekial	1:4-28	Also from within the whirlwind came the likeness of four living creatures. And this was their appearance: they had the likeness of a man. Each one had four faces, and each one had four wings. Their legs were straight and the soles of their feet were like the soles of calves' feet. They sparkled like the color of burnished bronze. The hands of a man were under their wings on their four sides; and each of the four had faces and wings. . . each had the face of a man; each of the four had the face of a lion on the right side; each of the four had the face of an ox on the left side; and each of the four had the face of an eagle.

Ezekial	10:9-12	And when I looked, there were four wheels by the cherubim, one wheel by each other cherub; the wheels appeared to have the color of a beryl stone. As for their appearance, all four looked alike--as it were, a wheel in the middle of a wheel. When they went, they went toward any of their four directions; they did not turn aside when they went, but followed in the direction the head was facing. They did not turn aside when they went. And their whole body, with their back, their hands, their wings, and the wheels that the four had, were full of eyes all around.
Revelation	4:6-8	And in the midst of the throne and around the throne were four living creatures full of eyes in front and in back. The first living creature was like a lion; the second living creature like a calf; the third living creature had a face like a man; and the fourth living creature was like a flying eagle. The four living creatures--each having 6 wings--were full of eyes around and within. And they do not rest day or night saying: "Holy, holy, holy, Lord God Almighty, Who was and is and is to come!"
Isaiah	41:9b-10	I have chosen you and have not cast you away: Fear not, for I am with you; Be not dismayed, for I am your God. I will strengthen you, Yes, I will help you, I will uphold you with My righteous right hand.
I John	3:1	Behold what manner of love the Father has bestowed on us that we should be called children of God!
II Corinthians	5:21	God made Him who knew no sin to be sin for us, that we might become the righteousness of God in Him.
Ephesians	5:15	Live life with a due sense of responsibility, not as those who do not know the meaning of life but as those who do.

Isaiah	58:10-11	If you extend your soul to the hungry and satisfy the afflicted soul, then your light shall dawn in the darkness, and your darkness shall be as the noon day. The Lord will guide you continually, and satisfy your soul in drought, and strengthen your bones; You shall be like a watered garden, and like a spring of water whose waters do not fail.
Mark and Matthew	10:44-45 and 20:27-28	And whoever of you desires to be first shall be slave of all. For even the Son of Man did not come to be served, but to serve, and to give His life a ransom for many.
Jeremiah	29:11-13	For I know the plans that I have for you says the Lord, plans for peace and not evil, to give you a future and a hope. Then you will call upon Me and go and pray to Me, and I will listen to you. And you will seek Me and find Me when you search for Me with all your heart.
Matthew	10:29-31	Are not two sparrows sold for a copper coin? And not one of them falls to the ground apart from Your Father's will. But the very hairs of your head are all numbered. Do not fear therefore; you are of more value than many sparrows.
Romans	8:37	Yet in all these things [tribulation, distress, persecution, famine, nakedness, peril] we are more than conquerors through Him who loved us.
James	1:12	Blessed is the man who endures temptation; for when he has been approved, he will receive the crown of life which the Lord has promised to those who love Him.
Ezekiel	13:22	Because with lies you have made the heart of the righteous sad; and you have strengthened the hand of the wicked, so that he does not turn from his wicked way to save his life.

II Kings   6:16-18   "Do not fear, for those who are with us are more than those who are with them." And Elisha prayed and said, "Lord, I pray, open his eyes that he may see." Then the Lord opened the eyes of the young man, and he saw. And behold, the mountain was full of horses and chariots of fire all around Elisha.

Questions to Ponder

Where does the Bible describe the orders of angels?
(Colossians 1:16, 1 Peter 3:22)
Discuss how order, hierarchy, and authority are important to God.

Where does the Bible describe the orders of demons?
(Colossian 2:15, Revelation 12:7-9)
Do you think order, hierarchy, and authority are important to Satan?
Satan upended God's authority, but do you think he insists that his underlings recognize his?
Do you see this same kind of hypocrisy in the world today? Can you give examples?

Where is the throne room of heaven described in the Bible?
(Revelation 4:2-11)
Could heaven be located in another dimension?
If not, where do you think it is? Or does it exist outside of time and space like God Himself?
Do you think humans can perceive it while still in the flesh, or do their spirits need to be free of the flesh in order to get to/see heaven?

Where is hell described in the Bible?
(Matthew 13:41-42)
Is this a physical place or a spiritual place?

In the book, Satan visits heaven. Is he allowed into heaven?
(In the book of Job, Satan comes before God during a convocation of the angels. He is referred to as the Accuser of the people, so he must come before God in order to do that.)

Satan is described as an angel of light.
What might he appear as to you?
How would he look and sound?

Why do you think Satan and his demons enjoy attacking you?
Do you think he would attack you more if you were advancing the kingdom of heaven mightily?
Could he use comfort and complacency as weapons against you?

Where is Jacob's Ladder mentioned in the Bible?
(Genesis 28:12)
Could it have been a portal to another dimension?
Does it still exist?

Are you sensitive to the spiritual world?
What can you do to be more in tune with it?

Trivia Question: Where is the name Adoram, the Seraph angel assigned to Rodney's case, mentioned in the Bible?
(2 Samuel 20:24 and 1 Kings 12:18)

Author Bio

Angelica Asher has been a published, non-fiction writer for over 20 years. She has written short fiction pieces and poems that have been printed in small publications. *The Book of Rodney* is her first novel. She maintains an author website at angelicaasher.com, a Facebook page at facebook.com/authorangelicaasher, a Twitter feed at twitter.com/Angelica_Asher, and Pinterest boards at pinterest.com/angelica_asher. She maintains discussions on angels and demons, the logistics of Heaven and Hell, and funny Christian kitsch items. Her writing is influenced by the works of Margaret Atwood, Terry Pratchett, Suzanne Collins, C.S. Lewis, Tina Fey, Frank Peretti, Douglas Adams, Jane Austen, and Charles Dickens.